BLIND PASS

TEAGAN HUNTER

Editing by Editing by C. Marie

Proofreading by Judy's Proofreading & Julia Griffis

Cover Design: Emily Wittig Designs

To my $80 Amazon office chair.
When I say you really carried the weight of this book, I mean it.
We had a good run.
#RIP

CHAPTER 1

RYAN

"To Hot Hockey Guy! And Hot Hitchhiker! He got the Cup, he got the girl, and he got the contract, baby!"

I toss back the shot of tequila like I'm a pro.

At this point, I just might be.

I've had quite a few drinks within the last hour, but it's fine. *I'm* fine. I have a good buzz going and I'm feeling amazing. Much better than I have in a long time.

I'm not thinking about my ex who is expecting a baby with someone else. And I certainly am not thinking about how the cost of my grandmother's assisted living facility went up and I have no idea how I'm going to pay for it now. How the salon I worked at let me go last week because they had to downsize. How I haven't told my best friend I'm really only one bad day away from being totally broke and sleeping on her couch.

Nope. Not thinking about any of that.

I'm just having fun in Vegas on a trip I'm not paying for and not worrying about any of it.

I glance over at my best friend, Harper, and her

ridiculously hot NHL player boyfriend, Collin, and frown.

I'm happy for Harper. Totally one hundred percent happy. Not at all jealous of the way her boyfriend looks at her. Just because I'm the one who is the hopeless romantic and believes in soulmates and Harper never has doesn't mean I should have been the one to find true love first.

Nope. Not jealous.

Their heads are bent close together and they're whispering. I just know it's about me.

Poor, poor, single-as-a-Pringle Ryan.

All lonely and drunk in Vegas.

So sad.

I'm certain that's what they're saying because I can read their lips and that's exactly what it looks like.

Somebody tugs on my hand, and I look over.

It's Rhodes.

Ugh, Rhodes. Mr. Grumpbutt.

He's always frowning and never having a good time. Not even now when we're in Vegas celebrating all kinds of exciting things like how his best friend won a Stanley freakin' Cup. Okay, fine—I guess he won it too because they both play for the Carolina Comets, but who cares! We're celebrating Collin, not Mr. Grumpbutt.

Rhodes tugs my hand again, and I look down at him.

He motions for me to get off the table I'm currently standing on. I shake my head because he's not the boss of me. If possible, his always frowning mouth pulls down even farther. He grabs my hand again.

I bend down so I'm at eye level and poke him right in the nose.

"No, thank you!"

Collin laughs, pulling my attention, and says something else to Harper.

Their mouths move again, and I squint, trying to see what they're saying now, but I can't because I'm upside down.

I'm upside down because I've been captured by a beast who won't let anyone else have a good time.

"Hey! You cranky hot giant! Put me down!"

He ignores me.

"Harper! Help!" I yell to my best friend.

Harper just shakes her head. "No! Go lie down—you're drunk!"

I gasp. "I am not!"

I'm not drunk, just buzzed. How dare she!

"Are too!"

"You traitor!" And she is. She's the biggest traitor ever. Who lets their friend get stolen away like this? I swat at the giant carrying me out of the club and away from my new best friend, alcohol.

"I thought you loved me!" I yell to my old best friend.

"I do!" the traitor yells back. "It's for your own good."

My own good? Is she nuts?! She's sending me off with a beast!

"He's going to kidnap me and hold me hostage in his castle!"

I swear I hear Rhodes mutter, "You wish."

I swat at him again for that comment, and he ignores my fighting once more.

When it's clear there's no use fighting him and Harper is *not* going to rescue me, I shake my fist at her and give in to my kidnapper as he carries me toward the door.

He doesn't stop moving until we're outside on the strip. He pulls me down his shoulder and sets my feet on the ground.

"Watch it, Mr. Handsy!" I say when his hands slide over my hips.

He rolls his eyes, grabs my hand again, and begins dragging me down the sidewalk.

I try to tug out of his grasp, but it's no use. He's too strong. Too strong and too muscly and oh wow…his back looks *really* hot in that shirt. It's all tight and maybe a size too small with the way it's stretching across him.

Rhodes keeps towing me along, and I keep letting him. But only because my feet are tired. Why did I wear stilettos again?

I crash into him when the big lug makes a sudden stop.

"Hey!" I brush my hair out of my face just in time to see him steer us into an old, fifties-style diner. "What are we—oh! French fries!" I reach for one and Rhodes smacks my hand away. "Ow!"

"Sorry," I hear him say.

"You most certainly are *not* forgiven."

"I wasn't apologizing to you. I was apologizing to the guy you just tried to steal food from. Come on."

More tugging and pulling.

Then pushing as he slides me into a booth. He leaves me sitting and walks up to the counter. He leans in close, talking to a server. I should make a run for it. He'd never catch me. There's no way.

But I'm too tired to move.

I slump onto the table, resting my chin in my palm, closing my eyes for just a moment.

I startle when Rhodes slides his big body into the booth across from me.

He's staring right at me, and I hate it because I like it.

I don't want to like it.

I look around, anywhere but at him.

"Ew. This place is hideous," I say. It's true. It's so ugly. Pastel blues and pinks cover the walls, and the décor is dated, and I hate it all. "Why are we here?"

"You need food."

Now it's my turn to frown. "I'm not hungry."

I'm not. I just want to go back to the club and dance and have fun and forget all about how sad and lonely I am.

Rhodes either didn't hear me, or he doesn't care. I wave my hand in his face, trying to get his attention.

"Hello, Mr. Grumpbutt, did you hear me? I. Am.

Not. Hungry." I enunciate every syllable extra clearly just in case.

"You're eating. You need to soak up some of the alcohol before I take you back to your room."

I rear my head back. "Um, I am *not* taking you back to my hotel room. We aren't having *the sex*."

"I didn't suggest having *the sex*," he mocks, lips twitching, "but it's nice to see where your mind goes. I said *I'm* taking you back to your room. For sleeping."

A pretty waitress sets down a plate of French fries and a giant, juicy burger.

"Eat," Rhodes instructs. "The last thing I need you to do is choke on your own puke."

I wrinkle my nose at his words but do as he says because the food *does* look really good.

I bite into a fry and moan. "Oh god. This is *soooo* good."

That stupid wrinkle that's always between his eyebrows deepens. "It's a fry. Stop moaning like you're having an orgasm."

"How do you know that's my orgasm sound?"

He ignores me and steals a fry from the basket. I let him, but only because I'm too busy shoving another one in my own mouth.

Before I know it, I've eaten half the basket and gulped a whole glass of water, which is saying something because I hate water.

I'm starting to feel much better, and the ugly diner isn't spinning nearly as much.

My phone buzzes in my purse and I pull it out.

It's my ex-best friend.

Harper: Don't be mad at me for sending you off with Rhodes.

Me: I'm mad. So, so mad.

Harper: Liar. Are you okay? Send me a pic so I know you're alive.

I snap a selfie and send it as proof of life. She sends me one back of her and Collin, and it makes me sad all over again.

"You okay?" Rhodes asks when he notices I'm frowning.

"No."

"No? Are you going to puke?" He looks alarmed.

I throw a fry at him. "No. I can hold my liquor just fine, thank you."

"Then what's wrong?"

I shrug. "I don't know. I'm… Have you ever been in love?"

He's taken aback by my question. "What?"

"Have you ever been in love?"

He scoffs and shrugs. "I guess you can call it that."

"Aww. You sound sad. Is that why you're grumpy all the time? Because you're sad because you got your heart broken?"

A scowl. "Sure."

"But she did break your heart, right?"

"She…dumped me, yes."

"Dumped you? But you're *you*. Hotshot NHL superstar. You're…" I gasp. "Oh no. You're bad in the sack, aren't you?"

His eyes narrow. "Shut up and eat your food, Ryan."

"I'm full."

"Too bad. Eat more."

I pick up a fry and nibble at it just to satisfy him. "What's her name?"

"Who?"

"The girl you couldn't make come."

"That's not…" He sighs, shaking his head as he settles back into the booth. "Brittney."

"Spears?"

I don't know why I said that. Of course it's not her.

"Kline."

I grab my phone, tap on Instagram, and type in her name. A few profiles pop up, but I know who it is the minute I see her.

I shove my phone in his face anyway just to be sure. "This is her?"

He glances at the screen for just a second and then away again like it's painful to look at her. He nods once.

She's gorgeous. Like supermodel gorgeous.

"She's really pretty. How long were you together?"

"A few years off and on. We've been more off recently though. But we'll be fine. We always are."

I listen to him as I keep scrolling through her photos. She posts a lot. Like three times a day.

But it's the post from two nights ago that really captures my attention.

"Is that why you've been so sad this weekend? Because she's engaged to someone else?"

His head whips my way. "What?"

He looks…sad. And mad.

He looks *smad*.

"Engaged."

"No."

"Yes. See."

I show him my phone and he snatches it out of my hand, looking at the image more closely. I might still be buzzed, but the emotions that run over his face are clear as day.

Anger.

Hurt.

Sadness.

Heartbreak.

"You didn't know?" I ask quietly.

He shakes his head, not taking his eyes off the photo. "No. I… Like I said…I thought we'd be fine. We're always…fine." He stares and stares, almost like he's willing whatever it is he's seeing to be something else.

But it doesn't change. She's engaged to someone else, and he's hurting.

And now I feel bad because he feels bad.

"Rhodes, are you—"

"This is my teammate."

"What?"

"The guy. In the photo—he's my teammate. Well, he *was* my teammate. I…I won a fucking Cup with this dude."

"Oh."

I don't know what to say. I don't know how to comfort him. I don't even know if he needs comforting because I don't really know him.

"Drink."

"What?"

He shoves my phone back to me. "Drink. I need a drink. A distraction. Dancing. Fun. *Anything.*"

His words surprise me. I haven't seen him drink more than one beer since we've been in Vegas, and he certainly hasn't been dancing. But right now, he looks like he could use more than one beer and the distraction.

"Please."

He's looking at me with a desperation I'm not sure I can ignore.

I shouldn't. I know I shouldn't. I've just started to sober up and there is nothing good that comes from drinking to forget.

But that hopeless, heartbroken look in his eyes

reminds me of the same hopeless, heartbroken look in *my* eyes.

We're kindred spirits. We *need* this. We need to let loose and forget our troubles. Forget the people who make us feel this way.

We deserve it.

"Okay," I say quietly. "Okay."

Rhodes rises from the booth and holds his hand out to me.

I slide my palm against his, letting him pull me up.

"Lead the way," I tell him.

And he does.

CHAPTER 2

RHODES

What's that saying? *Go big or go home?*

I went too fucking big.

I'm not a big party guy. I don't do loud and crazy. My idea of a wild night is drinking coffee and starting a *Lord of the Rings* marathon at 9 PM.

I'm boring and known for being a bit humdrum. I rarely let loose or get rowdy anywhere other than on the ice. I'm notorious for not being involved in many extracurriculars, and I don't do anything to draw any extra attention to myself.

Of course the one time I actually do, I fuck it all up majorly.

Me, my best friend and teammate Collin, and two other guys on the team I'm closest with—Miller and Lowell—had a weekend planned in Vegas. It was supposed to be a getaway just for us to celebrate winning the Stanley Cup. We were going to eat good food, drink a little booze, and bet way too much money on black.

Then Collin had to go and fall in love and bring his

girlfriend along. Naturally, she brought *her* best friend along because she was sad. Something about her being dumped and needing time away.

Collin made me promise I'd be "extra nice."

I highly doubt *this* is the kind of *extra nice* he meant.

I can feel the weight of it pressing down on me.

Or more specifically, I can feel the weight of it pressing down on my *finger*.

I peel open one eye and peek down at the gold band that feels like it weighs a thousand pounds. I press my palms into my eyes like I'm trying to rub away the memories of last night.

And really, I *am* trying to rub them away, because what the hell were we thinking? Why did we believe this was an okay idea? In what universe is getting married in Vegas a good idea?

It's not. It's an awful idea.

I should have taken Ryan back to her hotel room safe and sound just like I promised Harper I would.

But no. I had to drink away my sorrows and do something monumentally stupid.

I hate drunk me.

My head pounds—probably from the dehydration—but I don't dare get up for water.

Ryan's sleeping right next to me, and I'm not sure I'm ready to deal with her right now.

My wife.

My stomach turns at the thought.

We can get it annulled; I know that. And if I really want

to cause a scene, I'm sure I can get a lawyer involved because of us being so intoxicated. There's no way that was legal, no matter how much money (it was a lot) I threw at them.

I know deep down none of that matters though.

I can hear my phone buzzing on the bedside table, which can only mean one thing: I did not imagine us videoing the wedding and posting it online.

The nail is already in the proverbial coffin. There's no way I can walk this back now without looking like a complete fool. I can't just pretend it didn't happen and forget it.

I wish I could though. I wish I could forget it all.

Except for the part where she kissed me. The way her soft lips felt under mine. The way she melted into my touch. Those little noises she made as our tongues collided.

That I do not want to forget.

Or the part where we couldn't keep our hands off each other after that and spent the Uber ride back to the hotel with our mouths pressed together.

The moment I pushed open the hotel door, she stripped down to her underwear. Somewhere in my drunken brain, warning bells started to ring, and I had to put a stop to what we were about to do.

The look in her eyes when I turned her down about killed even drunk me.

But I'm glad I did it. I don't think I could manage the aftermath of that on top of everything else.

My phone buzzes again and Ryan groans. I should silence it before she wakes up.

As slowly as I can, I roll over and grab the phone from the table.

The first thing I catch sight of is a message from my mother.

Mom: ADRIAN TYLER RHODES! THIS HAD BETTER BE A JOKE!!

Shit. Middle name *and* double exclamations. That's how I really know I'm in trouble.

My eyes wander to the text from the general manager of the Carolina Comets.

David: I expect a phone call with an explanation.

I wince.

Fuck.

Usually, the organization is cool and doesn't give too much thought to what you're doing as long as you're not breaking any laws.

But when you start making headlines…they start caring. And I know this has already made headlines.

I click on the NHL app, and there it is, the first article of the day.

ADRIAN "THE BEAST" RHODES MARRIES BEAUTY INFLUENCER RYAN BELL

I cringe at the nickname the media won't drop. It was something I got back in my early days of hockey, and I haven't been able to live it down. I guess that's what happens when you take a skate blade to the face and get cut just an inch under your eye, through your lip, and down your chin.

The aftermath of that? Two surgeries, over a hundred stitches, and a big, ugly scar that's changed everything for me.

So, yeah, I guess I do look like a beast.

I'm sure tacking on about thirty pounds and six inches and constantly holding records for most hits in a season doesn't help.

I click away from the article just as a slew of texts come through, my phone buzzing like crazy in my hand. They're coming in so fast I can hardly keep up.

Britt: UR MARRIED

. . .

Britt: Is this sum joke????

Britt: Dammit! ANSWER ME! I've been calling you for 30 mins!!!!!

Britt: Srsly! Ur jealous I'm engaged to sum1 else, so u get married in Vegas to sum slut??? GROW UP!

Britt: So glad I don't have to waste NE more time on u

Britt: Hope she's worth it bc WE R DONE

I want to text her back and remind her that we were done when she let another man—especially my teammate—put a ring on her finger, but it's pointless.

More texts appear, some I really shouldn't be ignoring, but I do anyway, silencing my phone and setting it facedown so I can't see whatever else is coming through.

I should get up. I should deal with this whole mess.

Instead, I close my eyes and force myself to lie back down, hoping this is just one really bad nightmare.

CHAPTER 3

RYAN

I am a self-proclaimed hopeless romantic. I love everything about love. The meet-cutes, the soft touches, the shy smiles and subtle glances across the room as you begin to fall in love. The slow, sweet build into something epic. I'm even a fan of the ugly parts because, hey, that's what makes it so special, right?

I love watching romantic comedies and those damn tearjerker sappy love stories and reading romance novels. Valentine's Day is my favorite holiday, and I truly believe everyone has a soulmate out there waiting on them.

I naively thought I'd found mine with my ex-boyfriend, Steven, thought all the troubles we were going through were just ugly parts that were leading up to the big, beautiful ones.

But, man, I was *way* off.

Just hours before I hopped on a plane to Vegas with my best friend, Harper, and her NHL superstar boyfriend and some teammates of his, Steven texted me to tell me he was going to be a dad.

The only problem? I'm not pregnant.

It's safe to say our already troubled relationship was over after that.

I wish I could say I was responsible and did the mature thing, like send him a congratulations text or something like that.

But no.

I did what most heartbroken women would do during a night out in Vegas—I downed too much booze and danced with way too many men. I drank and drank and…well, I still felt like complete shit.

The biggest gut punch was having to watch my best friend and her boyfriend be happily in love all night. Don't get me wrong, I am *thrilled* Harper found love. I've known her since our first year of college, and I can't remember a time when she was this happy. She deserves it. Lord knows she's pushed it away long enough.

But seeing her and Collin together…I broke. It made everything feel ten times worse because I want what they have. I want that connection with someone else. I want that closeness. I want that commitment.

I just didn't expect it to come like this…

On cue, the massive arm around my waist tightens and the body it belongs to rolls, dragging me along for the ride. I push myself up, ready to climb off him, but freeze when his breathing changes.

I wait, holding my own breath, but he doesn't open his eyes or move.

He's still sleeping.

I peer down, studying the man I'm currently straddling. When he's awake, he's always sporting a scowl, and apparently, it's no different when he's sleeping.

But glowering or not, there's no denying one thing—he's beautiful.

I thought it the very moment I laid eyes on him. It took me so long to drag my eyes away that it made even *me* uncomfortable, which is a difficult feat. That's how striking he is.

His long, dark lashes brush against his cheeks. His ochre hair, which is in desperate need of a cut, is a complete mess, and there's a smidge of dried drool at the corner of his full lips.

"I can feel you *and* your tits staring at me."

I should be ashamed that I'm straddling him topless and staring at him, but I can't seem to find any fucks to give about the situation.

I used up a lifetime's worth of embarrassment last night.

"Your wonky one is looking right at me."

Even though he still has his eyes closed, I glare at him. "It is not *wonky*. It's just...bigger. And only slightly."

He peels his eyes open and glances down at my boobs, and I try not to squirm as he blatantly stares at me...especially not with his dick beginning to stir to life against my ass.

When he finally drags his eyes back to mine, he lifts a brow. "Why are you straddling me topless again? Was last night not enough for you?"

A frown pulls at my lips. As embarrassing as it sounds, I can't clearly remember what we did—or didn't—do last night.

His hazel eyes that are way too captivating fall to slits. "What? Upset you slept with the ugly guy on the team?"

Well, I guess that answers that question.

I try not to roll my eyes at his words.

He's always doing that, always calls himself ugly.

Any ugliness about him has nothing to do with how he looks. It's all in the way he acts.

Like a dick.

I try to push off him, annoyed. With him. With myself.

But he doesn't let me go.

I glare down at him. "What."

Not a question. More of a *Say something else asinine, I dare you.*

He doesn't take the dare.

Instead, he loosens his grip and lets me go. I roll off him and settle on the edge of the bed, facing away from him. I glance around, trying to find any clues as to what the hell happened last night after we got back to his room and I cracked open nearly all the bottles in the minibar and downed them. It's all coming up dark though.

The parts before that? Those are a little less fuzzy, though I wish they weren't.

I squeeze my eyes tight against the memories assaulting me and push them aside.

Clothes, Ryan. Put your damn clothes on and get out of here before you start freaking out.

I snap my eyes back open and continue my search. My bra is lying on the coffee table. My short black leather skirt is on the dresser, my burgundy velvet camisole is draped over the lamp, and there's one black stiletto on the chair. I have no clue where the other one is.

I didn't pay much attention last night—or at least I don't think I did—but this is easily the most extravagant hotel suite I've ever been inside. I guess it's a perk of my best friend dating an NHL player, I suppose. You start hanging out with them and getting to experience the finer things in life.

I do wonder how that lamp got broken though…

I push up off the bed and gather my things, including my phone that's sitting on the dresser too. I make the mistake of tapping the screen. It's filled with notifications. Like more than I've ever had before. Including one from my brother, which means the news must really be out because he's a world away and usually never all up in my business.

I power the device down, put off dealing with it, and begin to pull my skirt up my legs.

From behind me, I can hear him moving around and sighing. I wonder if he's checking his phone too.

"We didn't."

His voice is soft, a little scratchy from sleep and

probably the lack of hydration considering how much we drank last night.

I snap my gaze to him. A big mistake because the sheet is now around his waist as he sits on the edge of the bed, all those hard muscles he works overtime for on display.

I swallow the lump forming in my throat. "What?"

"Last night…we didn't sleep together."

He stands up, and I really wish he hadn't.

I wish he hadn't because now Adrian Rhodes, the top defenseman for the Stanley Cup-winning Carolina Comets, is standing in front of me naked.

Naked naked. Like he has no care in the world that his cock is staring directly at me.

And unfortunately for me, it's gorgeous.

Which is extra annoying because it's a dick. They can be pretty in passing, sure, but they aren't supposed to make my mouth water. Not like this.

He takes a step, and it bounces, knocking me over.

No, seriously—I'm now on my ass.

I am on my ass because I was so busy staring at his dick while I was trying to put on a freakin' leather skirt—why did I think this was a good idea?—and not paying attention to anything except the thing I want to lick.

Oh shit, am I still drunk?

Not lick—punch.

I want to punch him because Rhodes is a jerk. A complete ass. I mean, he just called my tit wonky. That's asshole behavior if I ever saw it.

He doesn't rush over to help me. He just stands there naked as the day he was born, watching me roll around on the floor like an idiot.

This is going swimmingly so far.

After taking entirely too long to do so, he finally asks, "Are you okay?"

I ignore him and continue trying to get my skirt pulled up. How I've managed to get myself all tangled and am *still* on the floor, I don't know, but I'm blaming Rhodes and his stupid, beautiful dick for this.

He lets out a hefty sigh as he pads across the room, his footfalls heavy on the carpet my cheek is currently attached to—and not in a fun way.

His hands curl around my waist and he plucks me off the floor with zero effort on his end.

He doesn't let me go. He holds me there, my skirt half around my thighs, my back to his still obviously naked front.

We don't move for a long time, and the reality of… well, everything, settles over us.

We didn't sleep together, but that doesn't erase everything else that happened. Hell, I would have preferred if we *had* slept together. That would have been better than what we actually did. Sleeping together is something I can forget and move on from. Not like it would be my first one-night stand.

But this?

I squeeze my eyes shut. Maybe we didn't do it. Maybe it was all just a really, *really* stupid dream. Maybe

I'll wake up at any moment and all of this will have been in my head. I'll be alone in my bed and I'll laugh and laugh because there is no way I could possibly be *this* dumb.

His grip tightens, and I look down at his fingers curled around me.

There it is. The evidence.

It wasn't a dream.

We're married.

I pinch my eyes shut in an attempt to hold back the tears that have started to sting my eyes.

We stand here for several moments, me trying not to cry, Rhodes holding me against him. I still don't have a bra on, and the longer we stand here, the more I'm unable to ignore his hardening cock that's brushing against the small of my back.

I want to crack a joke about his boner just to lighten the mood, but I doubt it would go over too well.

"Let go," I say softly instead.

He doesn't. He tugs me closer and rests his head against mine, breathing me in.

I let him.

I let him because deep down, I need this, and he knows I need this.

I hate that he knows.

"Please, Rhodes," I beg, unable to take it anymore.

With another sigh, he releases me, and I finish pulling up my skirt.

I grab my bra from the coffee table and slide it on,

followed by my shirt, all while ignoring him as he (finally) pulls on a pair of underwear.

I find my missing shoe—it was in the bathroom—and slip that on too.

Rhodes doesn't speak to me until my hand is on the door handle.

"Are you okay?"

I pause, my back to him, and let out a sigh.

It's the same thing he asked me before.

"I'm not sure," I tell him, because I'm *not* sure if I'm okay. I'm still trying to wrap my head around…well, everything that's happened over the last twenty-four hours. "We really…"

I don't finish the sentence. I can't.

He understands anyway. "Yeah."

"And it's…" I say, turning to him. He nods, confirming my worst fear, and I blow out a breath. "Okay."

"Okay?"

I laugh quietly. "I don't really know what else to say, Rhodes."

Another fucking nod. I'm starting to hate his nods. "Where are you going?"

"My room. To change. We have lunch with Harper and Collin and the guys before our flight tonight."

He looks upset by my words like he was expecting something else. Like he was expecting me to stay.

And really, I should. We have a lot to discuss. But if I don't get out of this room right now, I might break.

I can't break.

"Right. Lunch. With everyone."

His phone buzzes against the bedside table.

"Are they blowing your phone up too?" I ask.

"Of course. I have texts from Collin and your best friend."

I squeeze my eyes shut. "What…what are we going to tell them?"

"You mean how the fuck are we going to explain that we're married now?" He lets out a sardonic laugh. "I have no damn clue, but we should talk."

"I know. I just… Please, Rhodes. I…I need some space. Need to think."

He doesn't say anything else, and he doesn't try to stop me either.

I pull open the door and walk away from my husband.

CHAPTER 4

RHODES

It wasn't a dream at all.

The door clicks shut behind Ryan and I grab the thing nearest to me, chucking it across the room.

"Fuck!"

The scream echoes off the walls as I shove my hands through my hair.

"Fuck, fuck, fuck!"

I pull at the strands over and over again like I'm trying to pull out some magical fix for this fucked situation. But it doesn't work.

I need a shower. I need to think, need to clear my head. There has to be some work-around for this.

I head into the bathroom, and just as I flip on the water, there's a pounding on the door.

I sigh, already knowing who it is.

I ignore him too.

"Dammit, Rhodes, I know you're in there! Open the fucking door!"

He pounds on it, sounding like the police trying to break it down.

I switch off the water, not ready to face the music but needing to anyway. The last thing I want to deal with on top of everything else is security coming up here and busting my ass with a noise complaint.

I don't bother putting clothes on before pulling open the door to find a scowling Collin on the other side, hand raised, ready to pound again.

He narrows his eyes. "Tell me it's a joke."

Ignoring him, I turn on my heel, leaving him standing in the doorway staring after me.

He sighs, then follows me into the room. I bet if he could, he'd slam the door. He just stands there, hands on his hips like a grumpy old dad disappointed in his son, and that's so much worse than the door slamming.

I'm disappointed in myself too.

I grab a bottle of water from the fridge and twist open the cap, bringing it to my lips and chugging half of it in one go.

He continues to stand there staring at me, brows drawn tightly together.

I hold eye contact as I finish off the rest of the bottle, then crumple it up and toss it to the side.

"What?" I finally ask.

He shakes his head, scoffing. "I can't believe you. I cannot fucking believe you."

I can't believe me either. It wasn't exactly my finest moment.

"Why? How?"

I lift my shoulders. "It sounded like a good idea at the time."

"It sounded like a good idea at the time? That's the best you have?"

"Yes."

"Whose idea was it?"

"Both."

"Both of you? How? You were sober when you left with her and there is no way a sober you would have made that decision. I know you."

He's right. I wouldn't have.

"I was drunk."

"Is that even legal?"

"Highly doubt it, but…"

He cringes, and I know he's already seen the video too.

He nods a few times, understanding just how fucked up this whole situation is. He scrubs a hand over his face.

"I assume you saw the photo and that's what sparked this." It's not a question, more of a statement.

"Unfortunately."

When I saw the photo of Brittney and her engagement ring, I was hurt. But I was even more shocked when I realized it was my own former teammate in the photo with her.

I had no idea they even knew each other, though I guess I shouldn't be too surprised. Colter isn't the greatest guy out there. He has two baby mamas he hardly ever talks to, and last year he did nothing but pick fights with just about everyone on the team. I think nearly everyone breathed a sigh of relief when the Comets traded him earlier this summer.

"Colter is such a fucking piece of shit, and Brittney is...well, she's Brittney. *Of course* she'd do this to you."

Collin hated Brittney from the moment he met her, and I think it's safe to say he was right in his initial displeasure. He tried to warn me away several times, claimed she was never in it like I was and just wanted my money and the clout of dating a "celebrity." I dismissed him every time because I thought for sure one day we'd get over the back-and-forth of our off-and-on relationship and settle down.

Maybe if I had listened to him, I wouldn't be in this mess.

He doesn't understand though. It's easy for him to put himself out there. Sure, we both play pro hockey, so we have that going for us, but for me, it's more complicated than walking up to a hot chick and going, *"Wanna see my hockey stick?"*

Before my injury, I used to be confident, even a little cocky. Now? This scar is the first thing everyone sees when they look at me, and the first thing I see is the sympathy in their eyes.

You always think having a scar from doing something badass would be fun, but I promise you it gets old quickly.

The story gets old. The pitying looks get old. The recommendations of scar creams get old.

Collin…he doesn't know what that's like. He doesn't understand how hard it is to get somebody to look at me like I'm more than my scar. To find someone who isn't bothered by it and isn't embarrassed to be seen with me in public or pictures.

Brittney never cared about it. Or at least I didn't think she cared.

But going by the dude she had her arm wrapped around in the photo, she wasn't looking to settle down with an ugly guy like me.

Ryan, though, I *know* she doesn't care.

"I like your scar," she says, the smell of tequila hitting my nose. "It makes you look distinguished."

"I think you mean disfigured!" I shout over the loud music of the club. We've each had about four shots in the last hour, and I feel looser than I have in a long damn time.

She grabs my chin and pulls my face to hers, her green eyes that I'm really starting to like boring into me. "You're beautiful, Rhodes. Not despite your scar, but because of it."

It was the first time someone had ever called me beautiful.

I'm sure she didn't mean it. I mean, hell, she was three sheets to the wind.

But still…it meant something.

"What are you going to do?"

"What can I do? It's already out there. You know better than anyone how the internet is."

The year before last, we blew our chances at the Cup in the finals. Collin really blamed himself for what happened. After a night out at the bar turned into a brawl, it was Collin who paid the price. He was arrested for assault, and his name and mugshot were plastered all over the media. They dug deep into his past and found out he'd been arrested as a teenager too. It was a shitshow. The charges were eventually dropped, but the damage to his reputation was done. He spent the entirety of this past season rebuilding everything he had worked so hard for.

There's no way I can start this season with a similar cloud of chaos hanging over my head, and announcing an annulment after a crazy weekend in Vegas is exactly what that would be.

It isn't just about me. It would look bad on the organization and people would assume they can't keep their players in check. I don't want to be that guy who brings negative attention to the team.

"Think Coach is going to be pissed at me?"

"Coach? Think the entire fucking organization. Dealing with him was a cakewalk compared to that mess."

It's true. I remember hell raining down on Collin.

If you ask me, the media really screwed him over. His first arrest as a teen was for protecting his younger brother after some idiots were bullying him for being gay. His second arrest was for standing up to a drunken idiot putting his hands on a woman. He should have been hailed a hero, not a villain.

Needing more water, I reach back into the mini fridge, pop open yet another bottle of overpriced water, and guzzle it down.

I drag the back of my hand over my mouth.

"Getting drunk married, man? Really?"

Fuck me if that bile doesn't sting the back of my throat again.

I force it down once more and reach for my third bottle of water. I'm thirsty as fuck and need something to do with my hands before I punch a hole in the wall and have to pay for that too.

I can feel Collin's gaze on me the entire time.

"You can't annul it. It'll look bad on you both."

"I know."

I crumple the empty water bottle and toss it toward the others and then start hunting for my clothes.

This place is a wreck, and there's no doubt I'll be paying for the broken lamp—courtesy of Ryan's stilettos that she slung off without a care in her haste to undress—in the corner.

I doubt she remembers that either.

"You can't say it was just a joke because those records are going to be out there, and they *will* find them."

"I know."

"You can't—"

"For fuck's sake, I know! Do you think I haven't run everything through my head over and over again? I hardly slept last night because I was up worried and trying to figure out how in the hell I'm going to fix this. So save whatever bullshit you're about to spew for later."

He doesn't back away. Doesn't drop my heated stare.

All he does is stand there.

"Collin..." I pinch the bridge of my nose between my thumb and forefinger. "I fucking swear, I am about five seconds away from hitting you."

He sighs, then rubs his hand across the back of his neck, no doubt kneading away the tension bunching there. "I'm sorry, I just... She's Harper's best friend, you know? I feel protective of her."

I nod because I get where he's coming from. I've been feeling the same thing since the reality of this whole thing hit me. Ridiculous because we've only been married since last night.

"Are you going to stay married to her?"

I gulp back the lump that's formed in my throat because I don't have an answer to his question that's a good one.

There's a part of me that wants to stay married for the ease of it. I won't have to deal with the organization breathing down my neck or my parents' disappointment.

And in the very back of my mind, there's a small part of me that's scared this will be my only shot at marriage.

I know I'm not a catch. Sure, I have the pro-hockey-player thing, but that's it. I don't have looks. I don't have charisma. Most times, I'm an outright dick.

So, this? It could be my only chance.

I run a hand through my hair.

Fuck. I sound so soft right now. And crazy. Completely certifiable.

We can't stay married. There's no way…right?

"Rhodes?" he prompts again.

I blow out a long breath. "I don't know, man. I don't fucking know. Guess it's time I talk to my wife."

CHAPTER 5

RYAN

"Let's look on the bright side—at least the man I married is hot."

"Ryan Felicity Bell!" Harper admonishes. "How can you joke at a time like this?"

I lift my shoulders. "What am I supposed to do? Cry about it?"

"Anything would be better than just sitting here stoically like you have been for the past twenty minutes only to have the first thing you say be a damn joke."

Harper isn't usually the type to get upset so easily, but I can tell right now that she's mad.

What I can't tell is if she's mad *at* me or if she's mad at the situation *for* me.

When I left Rhodes in his hotel room, I headed straight for my own. I wasn't the least bit surprised to find Harper waiting outside when I arrived. Collin took one look at me and shook his head. He muttered something about Rhodes being an idiot and took off toward his floor.

He's been up there at least twenty minutes now, and I have no idea how that's going for them.

"Can you maybe not yell at me? I've kind of had a long night."

She winces. "I'm sorry, it's just…I'm worried."

"You think I'm not? It's already online. I'm sure everyone and their grandma knows about it by now."

Except for maybe my grandmother, but that's only because she doesn't know a tweet from a Facebook post.

Oh god—how am I going to break this news to her? I got married and she wasn't even there!

The reason I love love so much is because of her and my grandfather. They got married straight out of high school and were together for sixty years. I spent more time at their house than my own growing up, and watching them together was my favorite thing. Even after so long together, they were still in love like they were on their honeymoon. My grandfather brought home flowers every day and they danced in the kitchen after dinner every night.

They made me a believer in all things good.

When my grandfather passed away two years ago, it broke my grandmother. It was only a month later that she suffered a bad fall, broke her hip, and had a concussion. She wasn't comfortable living on her own after that and wanted to be around others her age.

She's been at an assisted living facility since, but she hates it. The nurses are awful and her roommate is intolerable on a good day, but it's all I can afford.

I don't want to add to her disappointment when she's already struggling so much.

"Have you talked to him?" Harper asks, pulling me from my thoughts.

"Not yet."

"You should."

"I know. I just…I needed some space. Clear my head, you know?"

"I get that."

Her phone buzzes in her hand and she looks down. I already know whatever she's looking at, it has to do with me. She doesn't frown like that for just anything.

"What is it?" I ask.

She tips the phone away from me. "Just more tweets."

"Ughhhh." I rub at my temples, my head pounding from the alcohol and probably a little from the stress of everything too. "All I wanted was one night of fun to forget about all the—"

I clam up, not finishing that sentence.

But Harper isn't letting me off that easy. "Forget about all the what?" Sharp as ever, her eyes narrow. "What don't I know, Ryan?"

I scrub a hand over my face, realizing I now have to confess my troubles. "Look, I was going to tell you after the trip, but…" I exhale. "I'm fucked."

She screws her lips up, confused. "O…kay?"

"I was let go at the salon last week."

"What?!" she explodes, pacing back and forth in front of me. "Why? What the hell happened?"

I shrug. "I guess the owner of the building came by to negotiate rent and it did not work out well for the salon. Macy needed to make some cuts, and since I'm the only one without any dependents, I was let go."

"But…but you're the best one there!"

"I know, but since I'm kind of a one-trick pony with my makeup skills and the other girls can do it all, it just made the most sense."

She shakes her head. "That's such bullshit."

"I get where she's coming from. Besides, she knows I have my income from my videos and whatever photography I'm able to sell."

"Still. It sucks."

"It does, but that's not even the worst of it. Rent hikes are a big thing this year because the cost of my grandmother's assisted living is going up too."

Her face falls. "No."

"Unfortunately, yes."

She comes to sit next to me, wrapping an arm around my shoulders. "Oh god, Ryan. I am *so* sorry. I… What are you going to do?"

"I'm not sure. I guess since I'm not at the salon anymore, I can make more videos."

"That's what you wanted to do all along anyway, so maybe this is a good thing?"

"True, but I wanted to get some savings built up a bit first, make a solid plan. You know better than anyone how much a small business can ebb and flow."

"So true."

Harper has a very…niche set of skills. She loves anything and everything horror related and decided to turn that into a very profitable business selling handmade items online. She makes home décor, trinkets, and even some props for movie sets that she ships all over the world. The things she makes are super creepy, but she loves it.

I always found it funny that we ended up becoming such great friends since we're total opposites. She's obsessed with the horror genre, and I jump at my shadow sometimes.

"Is that why you were drinking so much? Because you were upset?"

I nod. "Yes. It's dumb, but…between losing my steady income at the salon and the price of my grandmother's care going up, and then add in the whole Steven thing…well…" I shrug.

"You needed an escape. I get it. But can I just say maybe you went a bit too far?"

I laugh. "I think that's a fair assessment."

"What exactly happened? One minute he was tossing you over his shoulder to take you back to your room, and the next thing I know, you're married. How'd you go from that to the altar?"

"He started to take me back to the hotel but said he didn't want me to choke on my own puke, so he wanted to sober me up some first. Which I guess is sort of sweet in a Rhodes kind of way."

She laughs because she knows I'm right. Rhodes and

sweet do *not* go together.

"I kind of broke the news to him about that girl he's been seeing getting engaged." I cringe thinking about it. Nobody should find out that kind of thing via social media. "He said he wanted to get a drink and dance and have fun. After that, it's mostly blurry."

"Okay, for one thing, I cannot imagine Rhodes dancing. Like *at all.*"

When he first suggested it, I couldn't imagine it either. He's a big, scary-looking guy. No way could I picture him on the dance floor.

But I remember the feel of his hands on my hips as we danced together in the club. The way he held me to him like he never wanted to let me go.

He runs his nose along the exposed column of my neck.

"Are you sniffing me?" I shout.

"Yes. You smell incredible."

"I do not! I smell like sweat!"

He spins me around, my body crashing into his. He keeps his hands on my waist, pushing his knee in between my legs. My leather skirt rides up my hips and I'm practically exposed.

But I don't care.

Not when he keeps grinding against me and my clit grazes against his leg.

He drags his nose along my jawline, all the way up to my ear.

"You argue too much, Ryan. Someone ought to spank you for it."

"Are you offering?"

"Yes."

Images of Rhodes standing over me and my ass stinging red from his palm flash through my mind. A small noise escapes me, and I pray he didn't hear it.

I pull back, grinning up at him, trying to mask the fact that he's making me think some very naughty thoughts right now.

"Don't tease, Rhodes."

"Who said I was teasing?"

"You got this faraway look on your face. Were you thinking about Steven again?" Harper asks.

"Don't pretend you care about Steven."

"Oh, I don't. I hate that guy."

I laugh. I can't really say I blame her. He wasn't a great boyfriend. He never called when he said he would, he was always ditching me for his friends, and he always talked to me like he was better than me because he was a published photographer. No matter how hard I tried, I was never enough for him. I guess that's what I get for dating a self-centered artsy asshole.

"But I care about you, and I am sorry you're hurting because of him. I'm more than happy to help you bury his body though." I smile. "Did you ever find out how long they've been together?"

"I might have done a little social media stalking and saw on her Instagram that they met at his gallery opening a while back and hit it off."

Harper's brows crush together. "His gallery opening? You mean the one last year at the beginning of the season?"

I can't help but smile. "Look at you, talking all hockey seasons and stuff."

She blushes. "Stop it. You better not tell anyone I can talk sports now."

We can laugh about it now, but when Harper and Collin met on a dating app, Collin dropped so many hints about him being a hockey player. Harper being Harper, not knowing a damn thing about sports, didn't pick up on a single one.

Now I bet she can recite Collin's stats better than he can.

"Is that the same gallery opening though?" she presses.

I nod. "The same one."

"But that means…" Her eyes widen. "Does that mean he's been seeing her this *whole time*?"

I don't know, and I'm honestly not sure I *want* to know.

My gut is telling me yes though.

Based on the way Harper is looking at me, hers is saying the same thing.

She squeezes my hand again. "At least tell me he had a small dick."

My mind goes straight to the dick I saw this morning, which was definitely *not* small.

I push the thought away, hoping Harper doesn't see the blush that is no doubt stealing up my cheeks.

"Average, and there was a weird mole on the inside of his thigh that had more hair than my legs in the winter."

She wrinkles her nose, and I laugh.

Then somewhere along the way, my laughter turns to tears, and before I know it, I'm full-blown snot crying into Harper's shoulder.

I have no idea how long it takes for me to gather myself, but when I finally pull away, there is a definitive wet spot on her shirt.

"I snotted on you. I'm sorry." I wipe at it with a soft laugh, and my eyes instantly drop to the ring sitting snugly on my finger.

Harper notices and drags my hand into her lap, examining the ring Rhodes slipped on last night with a promise to love me forever. It's a simple slim gold band with a small heart engraved in the middle of it. Nothing fancy and nothing like how I imagined my wedding ring would look.

"It was something they had at the chapel," I tell her with a shrug. "He got one too."

"At least you didn't get it tattooed on," Harper comments with a laugh. "Or sleep with him."

Just the mere mention of a naked Rhodes has my mind drifting back to seeing him naked.

On one hand, I'm glad I didn't sleep with him last night. On the other…damn, what a missed opportunity.

Harper waves her hand around. "Okay, I know your horny face when I see it. What aren't you telling me?"

Busted.

I wring my hands. "I, uh, might have seen him naked."

"What! When? I thought you didn't sleep together."

"We didn't, but when I woke up this morning, all I had on were my panties and Rhodes was naked as the day he was born."

She lifts her brows but doesn't say anything. Probably because once upon a time—before I knew what a grumpy asshole he is—I thought he was hot.

Then he spoke, and all that flew right out the window.

There's a knock at my hotel door and I freeze, worried I conjured him up by thinking about his cock. I have this weird wave of wanting it to be Rhodes and simultaneously wanting it to be literally anybody else.

"It's just me," Collin says.

I exhale a relieved breath, and Harper gets up to let him in.

They stand in the door whispering for a few moments, glancing over at me from time to time. Subtlety is not their specialty.

Harper nods, then turns back to me. "We're supposed to meet Lowell and Miller for lunch, but I'm going to stay here with you."

"No!" I say, almost too quickly. "I mean, no. Go on ahead. I'll meet you down there."

Harper's brows pinch together. "Are you sure? I don't want to leave you alone."

"It's fine. I'm going to take a shower and map out the next big mistake I can make with my life."

Her face falls, and I laugh.

I laugh because if I don't laugh about it, I'm going to start crying again, and I don't want to cry in front of Collin.

Especially not when he's looking at me like he is. Like I'm some wounded animal.

I'm not wounded. Just stupid.

Really, *really* stupid.

"I swear, you're out to give me a heart attack this weekend," Harper mumbles as she crosses the room. She wraps me in her arms, and I hug her back. "We'll figure this out," she promises. "You're Ryan the Lion. You've got this."

I smile at the nickname she gave me in college. She was always the shy, awkward, quiet one, and I was always the exact opposite of that. She always said I was bold and brave like a lion, and the name kind of stuck.

"I'll be fine. I'll meet you down there in thirty," I tell her, hoping my words sound convincing enough.

She gives me one last long, sad look, then shuffles out the door with Collin. Like the amazing boyfriend he is, he looks equally concerned about my well-being.

The moment the door clicks shut, I fall back on the bed, exhausted from last night and all the emotions of the day so far. I glance over at the clock and note that it's only eleven. How can it only be eleven?

Twelve hours.

That's how long I've been married. Twelve hours. And I remember this because we made sure to say our vows at 11:11 PM.

I thought it was romantic. Something out of a fairy tale.

I believe in love, and I believe in fairy tales, but this?

This is no fairy tale.

It can't be. Not when it makes me feel this way, sick to my stomach with dread.

Maybe that's just the alcohol though. I should probably eat something, but just the thought of food makes me want to hurl.

A bath—that's what I need. If I'm quick, I can take about a fifteen-minute soak to let all the tension out of my body.

I'm just about to push up from the bed when the sound of a key sliding into the electronic lock stops me in my tracks.

I'm sure it's just Harper checking in on me. We always make sure to exchange room keys just in case, but this is the first time I'm regretting that choice.

I just want to be left alone. I want to sit in a tub of hot water and think about how the hell I'm going to get out of this mess I'm in. Hell, maybe I'll order room service and charge it to my *husband's* room. I can do that, right? What's his is mine and all that.

The door opens, and I sigh. "I told you, Harper, I'm fine."

"Yeah, well, I'm not. We need to talk."

It's not Harper. It's Rhodes.

And he doesn't look happy.

"Got a moment to chat, *wife*?"

CHAPTER 6

RHODES

"I don't know where she is. She said she'd meet us here, but she's not answering her phone."

I know because I tried it too.

Is she trying to bail on me?

"Give her some space, man. Maybe she just needs time to process." Collin places a hand on my shoulder, and I shake it off.

I also needed time to process, but Collin had no issue with dragging my ass down here for lunch with Lowell and Miller. If I have to be here and face everyone right now, she damn sure has to be here too.

We both fucked up last night. I'm not going to let her hide just because she's too embarrassed to own up to her mistakes.

Without another word, I spin on my heel and head for the elevators. Harper calls out after me, but I don't bother stopping. I'm a man on a mission, and it's time I had a chat with my wife.

I take the elevator up to the thirty-fifth floor and let myself in with the key card I have.

I hear her sigh as I push open the door.

"I told you, Harper, I'm fine."

"Yeah, well, I'm not. We need to talk. Got a moment to chat, *wife*?"

I say it just to test her, and to her credit, she doesn't flinch.

Nor does she look all that surprised to see me.

"How did you get in here?"

I hold up the card. "You dropped this in my room."

That's a lie. The first thing I did when Collin finally left my room was go to the front desk and get a replacement. They really have some shitty service in this hotel. I barely had to talk my way into getting it.

"How convenient."

"Sure was." I shut the door behind me. "We need to talk."

"You already said that." She pushes off the bed with a sigh, heading into the bathroom.

She gathers her long, honey blonde locks and twists them up into a messy bun and then bends over the garden tub. She hits a few contraptions and switches on the water. She reaches for a bottle of bath salts sitting in the corner and dumps the entire thing into the bottom of the tub. Another bottle of the stuff is emptied, and before I know it, she's hooking her thumbs into the waistband of her skirt and tugging it down her legs.

Her shirt is lying on the floor next to it before I can

even grasp what I'm seeing.

"What are you doing?" I finally manage to ask.

"What does it look like? I'm taking a bath."

She says it so calmly, like she's not just undressing in front of me and slowly killing me.

"Nothing you haven't seen before."

"I told you we didn't sleep together."

Quite frankly, it's pissing me off that she thinks I would take advantage of her when she was drunk. I might have been shit-faced too, but that's not the kind of man I am.

"We might not have slept together, but I clearly undressed in front of you at some point last night, so unless you're unable to handle seeing some boobs..."

Some boobs? She says it like she doesn't have an incredible rack.

I try my damnedest to look away when she reaches behind her back and unsnaps her bra, but like a flustered eighth-grader who is seeing tits for the first time, I look at the mirror, as if that's going to magically change anything.

She doesn't back down, doesn't call me out on it.

Our eyes collide in our reflections as she drags her bra down her arms and drops it to the floor. She's back to the same state she was in when she was straddling my waist this morning.

And just like then, my cock springs to life.

Her perky tits are hanging free, her nipples hard and in perfect proportion to the rest of her boob. Fuck, I want to taste them. So damn badly. I had to fight so hard not to reach up this morning and pull her breast into my mouth.

Just like I have to fight the urge right now.

She's beautiful. There's no denying that. I thought it the first moment I saw her.

But it's more than just her looks that make her beautiful. It's the unabashed confidence she has in herself. The way she presses her shoulders back and meets my stare head-on, almost daring me to touch her.

I admire that about her.

Her watchful gaze skates across our reflections and lands on the one thing I hate the most—my scar.

It's only then that I finally turn away from her and not-so-subtly adjust my hard dick.

She turns off the water, and I hear her step into the tub.

"You wanted to talk, so let's talk."

I face her again just as she sinks under the bubbles, covering everything I so desperately wish I could see again.

Leaning against the bathroom counter, I cross my arms over my chest, watching her. Her eyes are closed, and to most, she might look at ease. But I can see the way her jaw is tensed and how her lips are tugged down in the corner just the slightest bit.

"Last night was—"

"A huge mistake? Like monumentally huge? The biggest regret of my life?"

Even though I'm harboring those exact feelings, there's something about the way Ryan says it that cuts just a little bit.

Could it be because she's embarrassed by me? That out of all the people she could have done this with, I had to be the guy?

"Yeah, that."

She lets out a humorless laugh and sinks lower into the tub, keeping her eyes closed. "We're trending on Twitter, you know."

Fuck. Of course we are.

Which means it's as bad as I thought.

"What are we going to do?" She whispers the words, but I hear them just fine across the bathroom.

"I think we should stay married."

Just as fast as the statement leaves my mouth, she's scrambling around the tub, completely shocked by it.

I'm shocked by it too.

"Are you insane? We can*not* stay married."

The way she says it makes it sound like she's disgusted by the idea, which just pisses me off.

"We barely know each other, Rhodes!"

"I guess you should have thought about that last night before you said I do."

"I was *drunk*."

"So was I, but you don't see me running from my mistakes." *Probably because I'm an idiot, but…*

She shakes her head. "You're nuts. We can't stay married."

"Why not?"

"Why not? More like why *should* we?"

Marriage has always been something important to me. It's not like I've ever been in any rush to get down the aisle, but it's never been a thing I've not taken seriously either—at least not until last night.

I've seen other guys in the league not take it seriously too many times to count. They screw women all over the country and show off that Instagram-worthy life at home, pretending they aren't sticking their dicks in anything that walks the moment they are away. It's a joke to them.

But not for me. It means something, a lifetime of sticking by someone who complements you in all the best ways. It's a true, honest commitment. It definitely does not mean a quickie in Vegas with an Elvis impersonator at the ready to help you exchange your vows. We didn't go that route, thank fuck. Apparently even drunk we have *some* class when it comes to a Vegas elopement.

I'm already that guy with the ugly scar. I can't also be that guy who got married in Vegas.

And more than that, I don't *want* to be that guy.

"Because you need me, and I need you."

"I don't need you."

I laugh darkly. "Oh, but you *do* need my help. I might have been drunk last night, but I distinctly remember you telling me about losing your job and your troubles about your grandmother's assisted living situation."

Her mouth drops open. "I told you about that?"

"Yes. How you're barely hanging on paying for it and you want nothing more than a Prince Charming to come and save you. Ring any bells?"

It's clear that it doesn't.

But I remember it very well.

She cried for a good twenty minutes about it. I remember because if there's anything in this world that I hate, it's lady tears. Well, I also hate having to block shots going a hundred miles an hour on the ice, but I fucking hate lady tears too.

I've only seen my mother cry in a handful of instances, and it has about killed me every one of those times.

"Is that…is that why we got married?"

"I…"

Fuck. Collin asked me the same thing.

Why'd we do it?

As sad as it sounds, I don't know.

I know I was upset about Brittney. I know I wanted to forget her engagement to Colter and maybe even show her I was over her. But I don't think that's the reason we did it. It doesn't *feel* like the reason we did it.

But I was drunk, so what do I know.

I just know that try as I might, I can't remember, and I'm not sure whether that's a good or bad thing.

"I, uh… Well, I don't actually know the exact reason we got married." I rub at the knot forming at the back of my neck. This shit is stressing me out. "I don't remember much leading up to it."

She seems sad yet relieved to hear that. "Well, at least we're on an even playing field there." She shakes her head. "I can't believe I told you about my grandmother. Not even Harper knows the full extent of it."

"Well, believe it. You did. And I can help you with it if you help me with my problem."

"What problem?"

I wave my hand between us. "This. There's an expansion team coming in out west, and I don't want to be on the chopping block for it. If I'm doing stupid shit like this during the offseason, it's not going to look good. I'll be a liability and they won't keep me, and I'd really like to stay."

It's not a lie at all. Everyone knows they're on thin ice this upcoming season.

"Not to mention it's already out there in social media land and everyone knows the internet is forever," I continue. "I'm sure the entire Comets organization knows about it already, so I'd have to deal with that shitstorm too. And then there's the whole letting-my-parents-down thing that I'd really like to not do."

"You can't be serious about this."

I don't say anything because as much as I don't want to be, I *am* serious.

Her face falls, and it finally dawns on her that I'm not kidding at all. "Rhodes…"

She clamps her mouth shut, rolling her lips tightly together as she studies me, mulling it all over in her head.

I wait. I wait for her to tell me to go fuck myself. I

wait for her to leave me high and dry to deal with this myself.

I wait for her to tell me she can't possibly imagine being married to a man like me.

Her lips pop free and I brace myself, ready for it.

"Okay."

I balk at her response. "Okay?"

She nods. "I'll do it. But we need to make a plan."

"A plan?"

"Yeah, like how long are we going to stay married? How long are we going to keep this charade going?"

I run my hand over my jawline, scrubbing at the stubble that's formed in the last twenty-four hours. I don't typically keep any facial hair because it draws too much attention to my scar, but I couldn't be assed to shave this morning. Now I'm glad for the distraction.

I really haven't thought this far ahead. I just figured we'd ride out the social media storm for a few months and then figure things out from there, but dealing with everything during hockey season…well, I can't do that.

"The season maybe? I have to focus on hockey, and I can't deal with a divorce and other drama in the middle of that."

She scoffs. "You say that like I'm going to drag you through the mud and take you for all you have like some kind of gold-digging monster."

I don't refute her claim because I'd be lying if I said I wasn't a little worried about that. I know Ryan, but I don't *know* Ryan. I have no idea what she's capable of, and people do some sketchy shit when they are desperate. Since I don't have a way out of this situation other than seeing it through, I'm going to protect myself as much as I possibly can, which means focusing solely on my divorce when it comes time for that.

Divorce. The word tastes awful in my mouth.

It's crazy to think we just got married last night and we're already talking about it like we're discussing what groceries we need to buy.

But that's what we have to do, isn't it? We have to keep this professional and businesslike. The last thing we need to do is bring any sort of emotions into this mess.

"And if you make it to the playoffs? That'll be like a year…"

Doesn't she know she's going to jinx it by implying we won't make it?

"*When*," I correct her. "If you're going to be married to a hockey player, you should know we're a bit superstitious. So, *when* we make the playoffs, we'll reevaluate things."

She laughs humorlessly. "Reevaluate things. I can't believe that's how I'm talking about my marriage."

I can't either.

"What are we going to do about our families?" she asks.

I groan just thinking of how my mother is going to go full-blown batshit. "Make them believe it, I guess. What about your parents? Will they care?"

"They aren't…part of my life. It's just me, my older

brother who is off doing Marine things in Okinawa, and Grams."

The nonchalant way she says it makes me feel uneasy and a little sad for her. My family isn't perfect by any stretch of the imagination, but I couldn't fathom not having them in my life.

My mom is loud and a little overbearing at times, and my dad can kind of get on my ass about my hockey stats, but they love me and support me. I don't know where I'd be without them.

"All right," I say. "We lie, then."

"We lie," she agrees. "Other than Harper and Collin, nobody can know this is fake. We have to play it up if we want to make it believable. Your family, teammates, your coaches—nobody can know the truth. Can you handle that?"

Handle that? Please. I'm the king of faking it until I make it.

"The GM might kill me, but it shouldn't be a problem."

"Maybe you should get my name added to your life insurance policy before we go back, just in case."

Oh look, she's got jokes.

"Do Lowell and Miller suspect anything?" she asks.

"I don't know. I haven't talked to them. Lowell certainly isn't stupid, so I'm sure he knows something is up. Miller, on the other hand...well, he's Miller."

I love the rookie. He has some seriously sick hands

out on the ice and is a big reason our team won the Cup, but he can be a bit dense sometimes.

Ryan laughs, understanding what I'm getting at, and it's the first real laugh I've heard from her since we got into this mess. I don't hate the sound of it.

"If we're going to pull this off, I think it goes without saying we won't be seeing other people during this whole sham of a marriage."

She eyes me, waiting on my answer anxiously. I want to be annoyed that she would even suggest I'd step out on her, but to be fair, with the way we got married, it's clear I'm not the best at making decisions.

"Of course not."

"Good, good." Her shoulders sink with relief, and she clears her throat. "And our living situation? What about that?"

"We'll live at my house, of course."

The look she gives me says she wouldn't share a room with me even if she had to.

I don't know why I say that last part. It just comes out, but I realize I mean it.

"You have a house?" she asks, and I drag my eyes away from her body. If she noticed me staring, she doesn't call me out on it.

"Yeah, where did you think I live? In a box somewhere?"

"Or hell." I ignore her jab and her proud smile. "Possibly even in an apartment. Some bachelor pad for sure."

"No apartment. No bachelor pad. I just bought a three-bedroom house over in Grandview Hills."

She lifts her brows at the name of the neighborhood, which is known for being a bit ritzy. I didn't choose the place because of that; I just liked the privacy that came with it.

I'm not the type to have my business and my name splashed across the headlines. For someone who plays a professional sport, I live a low-key life. With this scar marring my face, I already give people enough reason to pay attention to me. I don't need to add to that, which of course makes this whole situation even worse. I have a feeling I don't even want to know what they're saying about us online right now.

"What do you need three bedrooms for? It's just you, isn't it?"

I lift my shoulders. "I like having the space, especially when my family comes to visit."

Which they do often, and that's going to suck.

"Are you close with them? Your family, I mean."

"Yes. They gave up everything for me. I owe my entire career to them, and I make sure they know it, flying them out for games as often as possible."

She nods once, her eyes full of something I can't quite place my finger on. "Your place it is, then."

"All right. Any other stipulations?"

"Yes. I want my own bedroom, there will be *no* PDA, and I'm not taking your last name."

"Even if this were a real marriage, I wouldn't expect

you to. It's your name—you do what you want with it." Her eyes widen at my response, surprised by it. "Did I say something wrong?"

"No." She shakes her head. "I just thought you might argue. That seems to be your thing with me. I say something, you say something snarky back, then walk away all hot and grumpy."

I lift a brow at her choice of words. "Hot and grumpy?"

She rolls her eyes and sinks lower into the tub. The bubbles are nearly completely gone, and if I were standing any closer, I could see everything.

I really want to see everything.

"If there's nothing else, you can leave now. I'd like to finish my bath in peace."

"Actually, there is one other thing I'd like to discuss."

"Of course there is," she grumbles, closing her eyes and relaxing into the water that I'm sure is cold by now.

I stalk across the bathroom, not stopping until I'm hovering above her. I was right; I *can* see everything. Every dip and every curve.

My fingers itch to reach out and touch her because I can clearly remember how every inch of her feels under my fingertips. How my rough palms dug into her soft flesh when I wrapped my hands around her waist and held her against me.

She's fucking stunning.

From the way her breathing picks up, I know she can feel my eyes on her body. And with the way her nipples pebble just under the surface of the water, I know she likes it.

"Sex."

Her eyes fly open. "Excuse me?"

"Sex. We'll be together for a year. You're going to want it."

She snorts, turning her nose up at me. "With you? Not likely."

Her words sting, but I'll never tell her that.

I lean down, resting a hand against the side of the tub. "Trust me, you will."

I place a few fingers on her knee that's poking out of the water. She gasps just from the miniscule touch. I laugh darkly as I walk my fingertips down her thigh and underneath the bath water, not stopping until I'm dangerously close to her pussy. So close I can feel the heat coming off her.

Her legs part, begging me to touch her, and I'm not even sure she notices it.

"But, Ryan?"

She makes a noncommittal noise, her eyes drifting shut as I inch closer and closer.

"It's not going to happen."

Without warning, I yank my hand from the water and flip the button on the drain.

I shake my wet hand over the tub and grab the nearest towel, tossing it at her.

"We have lunch plans. Get dressed, *wife*."

CHAPTER 7

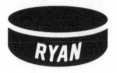

RYAN

Are you allowed to hate your husband when you've been married for less than twenty-four hours?

If so, I'm pretty sure I hate Rhodes.

I hate the way he stood over me, staring down at me with those hungry hazel eyes of his. The way he drank in my body that I know he could see through the cloudy water.

But what I hate most of all is the way my body reacted to his gaze.

Maybe I was wrong. Maybe it's not a good thing that my husband is hot.

He's right—a year is a long time to be celibate. It's going to be hard, but after that little stunt he just pulled, I'm determined to prove him wrong.

I won't want him. I *can't* want him.

Ugh, I can't believe I've agreed to this. I have to be crazy, don't I?

It was hard to tell him no when he was looking at me like he was. I know he's worked hard for this career. Hell, he took a damn skate blade to his face and still kept pushing to make his dreams happen. I don't want some drunken mistake—especially since it's me—to put all that at risk for him.

He's not the only person I'm doing this for, though.

My grandmother took me in and raised me when she didn't have to. She gave up so much in her life for me. The least I can do is give up a year of mine to repay her and make sure she's comfortable living out the rest of her life.

One year, and he'll be gone most of it because of hockey season. I got this.

I can see him from where I'm at. He's currently sitting on the end of my bed, scrolling through his phone while waiting for me to finish getting ready for lunch.

I get where he's coming from when he says we need to go, need to show a united front. But I don't want to go. I don't want to face my mistakes from last night. I suppose since we're going to be running this farce for an entire year, we might as well start now.

"That video is…wow."

I poke my head around the bathroom door. "You're looking at my Instagram account?"

"Figured I should learn a few things about my *wife*. Your account is popular."

I hate the way he says wife—like it's a curse word.

"It's nothing. I'm small potatoes compared to some creators."

"I'm pretty sure you have more followers than our team's account."

It almost sounds like there's a little bit of pride in his voice, and I don't know how to feel about it.

Unless it's coming from my grandmother, pride isn't something I'm used to.

"It's nothing," I say again. "I have more followers on YouTube anyway."

"Do you make money doing this?"

My hackles rise at the judgment in his tone.

I get it. Social media is the worst sometimes, and content creators get a bad rap. It's not like I set out to have this as my career though.

In college, Harper and I took a special effects makeup class because we thought it would be fun. I fell in love instantly and became obsessed with watching makeup videos on YouTube. Before I knew it, I was making my own. Ugh, those earlier videos are *awful.* Poor lighting, poor editing, and even poor makeup. But with practice, I got better, as did the quality of my videos, and eventually, I garnered some attention for turning myself into different celebrities, creatures, and a few different Disney characters. Things took on a life of their own after that.

I was able to monetize my channel and started to bring in an extra hundred dollars a month. Now, it's in the thousands. It's nothing compared to what some beauty gurus make, but it's generally enough to cover my grandmother's care, which is *not* cheap. My parents aren't going to help with the cost anytime soon and my older brother lives a whole word away in Japan and is busy being a Staff Sergeant in the Marine Corps, so if this is what I have to do in the meantime to pay for it, I'll do it —Rhodes' judgment be damned.

"Not that it's any of your business, but yes, I do."

He lifts a challenging brow. "Actually, it *is* my business, *wife*."

I glare at him. "Well, in that case, since you're so worried about my finances, I'll make sure to bring my bank statements to lunch for you to look over. We can cry about my student loan debt together."

He narrows his eyes, not appreciating my sarcasm.

"You still have student loans?"

"Yes."

"I can pay those too."

My stomach drops at his suggestion. "Is this some kind of *Pretty Woman* situation to you? You're not paying my student loans."

"But you're fine with me paying for your grandmother?"

I'm not fine with it. Not at all. I wish I could be the one to take care of her, but I'm also not stupid. I'm not going to let an opportunity like this pass me by.

I've already been running the numbers in my head. If I work my ass off to post more content over the next year and save my money wisely, I should be able to pay off the remainder of my student loans, and that'll take away a big burden.

"You're not paying my student loans," I say again.

He grits his teeth at my response, not looking the least bit satisfied. "Fine."

"Fine. Anything else, *husband*, or can I finish getting ready?" I toss the word back at him with just as much disdain as he's been serving me.

"I don't want our life together on social media."

His answer is quick and cagey, his whole demeanor changing. It's clear he's uncomfortable with the idea.

My eyes drift toward his scar. I suspect that's his reasoning for not wanting to be in the spotlight.

When he realizes what I'm looking at, he abruptly rises to stand, his giant six-foot-four frame towering over me as he looks down his nose at me.

"We're late."

It's all he says, dropping the conversation before I have a chance to answer him.

Okay, then.

I step back into the bathroom, apply one last swipe of mascara, and give my hair a fluff, then turn off the bathroom light.

"Let's go," I say, meeting his challenging stare head-on.

I do my best to ignore the way his eyes trail over my body. Just like I do my best to ignore the way my nipples pebble under his gaze.

I grab my purse off the dresser and slide the strap over my shoulder, following him out the door.

The ride in the elevator seems unusually long, and

that same tension that was in the room follows us through every floor. He stands opposite me, hands shoved in his pockets, eyes never leaving mine.

It's like we've entered a staring contest, and at this point, I have no idea who is winning.

When we arrive at the main floor, he blinks, looking away first. I don't bother trying to hide my victorious smirk.

His fingertips graze the small of my back as we shuffle out of the elevator. Just as quickly as they make contact, they're gone, and it's strange because I miss them instantly.

Just as we're about to cross into the restaurant, his lips brush my ear, sending a shiver down my back.

"Last chance," he whispers, and I hear the challenge in his voice.

He thinks I can't do this. Thinks I can't handle this.

He has no idea just how strong-willed I am.

It's only a year, I remind myself. *One year. That's it. You can do this. Besides, it's not like my heart is on the line or anything. Piece of cake.*

"I'm not backing out."

His lips twitch, almost like he wants to smile. But he doesn't. *Of course* he doesn't.

He just nods once and then straightens to his full height. "Let's do this, then."

Rhodes steers us through the restaurant toward the back where we are greeted with a loud, obnoxious, attention-drawing cheer from none other than Miller.

"Woo! Yeah! Congrats to the newlyweds!" He sticks his fingers in his mouth, letting out a whistle. It's obnoxious and does nothing to help the hangover headache I have.

Everyone's eyes are on us, and it's not like the restaurant is empty. A few people whisper behind their menus, no doubt recognizing Rhodes.

I could maim Miller for his antics, and by the look on Rhodes' face, he feels the same.

Lowell grabs his shoulder, pulling him back down to his chair. "Shut up, you idiot."

"What? I'm just happy for the newlyweds." Miller shakes off Lowell's attempt to rein him in and rounds the table, wrapping his arms around Rhodes, patting him on the back. "So happy for you, bud."

Rhodes gives him an Oscar-worthy performance and hugs him back, even going as far as to pat him on the back.

"Thanks, man. Appreciate it."

Miller lets him go, and then it's my turn for a hug. He wraps me in his arms, his big body engulfing my small frame.

I meet Rhodes' gaze over Miller's shoulder, and he looks…angry?

That's not at all what I was expecting.

"I was hoping I'd have a shot with you," Miller says as he lets me go. He claps Rhodes on the shoulder. "But I guess that's out of the question now."

The sound that leaves Rhodes is nothing short of a growl.

An actual fucking growl.

I don't know how to feel about that.

Miller just laughs and heads back to his seat. Lowell rises from the table and heads our way.

He gives Rhodes an almost imperceptible headshake but hugs him for show. I can't read his lips, but I know whatever he whispers to Rhodes, he does *not* like.

Lowell frowns down at me, and I somehow feel like I've disappointed my dad. Ridiculous because he's only a couple of years older than me, but it's the way he carries himself that makes me feel so small. No wonder he's the team captain. He's scary as hell.

He gives me a quick hug, and we all take our seats. Rhodes and I are directly across from Harper and Collin.

Harper gives me a sad smile and mouths, *You okay?*

I shrug because…am I okay? I don't know.

Unable to stand the way she's looking at me—like I'm a skittish kitten about to run away—I turn my attention to the menu in front of me.

Miller turns to Rhodes. "Dude, I know I haven't seen you in a couple of weeks, but I had no idea you two were dating, and I sure as shit had no idea it was this serious." He gasps. "Oh, fuck. Did you get her pregnant?"

The way he whispers *pregnant* makes me laugh, causing Rhodes to look over at me. I ignore him.

"Shut the fuck up, Miller," Lowell chides.

"What? It's a genuine question. How else do you explain a shotgun wedding?"

Alcohol. Lots and lots of alcohol.

"Besides, it's not my fault I have pregnancy brain. My sister is knocked up, and babies are all I can think about."

"That's terrifying on many levels," Rhodes comments, and I have to agree.

"That's not how pregnancy brain works, you moron." Lowell shakes his head. "And you don't just ask women if they're pregnant. That's like rule number one in life."

Miller's cheeks turn a deep shade of red as he peeks over at me. "Sorry."

I jump a little when a hand wraps around mine. Rhodes laces our fingers together, rubbing at the ring sitting on my finger. The same one he placed there last night. "Not pregnant. We've kept it quiet, but we just couldn't hold it in any longer." He says it with such sincerity that even *I* almost believe it. He grins over at me. "When you know, you know, right, *babe*?"

Ugh—babe. Gag me with a spoon.

Steven used to call me that, and I hated it then too.

"That's right, *honey*." My words drip with just as much sarcasm as his.

His eyes flare at the pet name.

Good. Looks like he hates them too.

"Aww," Miller says, "this is some shit right out of a romantic comedy."

Rhodes and I exchange a glance because he has no idea just how close to the truth he is.

Our server comes by and grabs our orders, saving us from answering more questions about whether I'm knocked up or not. The conversation around us flows easily, Miller moving on from grilling us about our newfound love.

It's not until our breakfast arrives that I realize I'm still holding Rhodes' hand.

I think out of all the crazy things to happen so far this weekend, the level of comfort I find in his touch might just be the hardest pill to swallow.

CHAPTER 8

RHODES

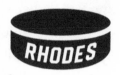

After lunch, we all went our separate ways. I didn't even argue with Ryan when she said she was heading to her own room. We should probably spend some time getting to know one another, but I needed a break.

I needed a break because sometime during lunch I realized it felt a little too comfortable to be sitting next to Ryan. That realization came when I noticed I held her hand far longer than I needed to.

It felt…good. Easy.

Almost…right.

And that made me want to hurl my lunch back up, so I hid in my room like a total wuss.

I sacked up and finally gave my general manager and coach a call to set up plans for a meeting first thing tomorrow morning so we can go over a press release. To say they were surprised by my sudden nuptials would be an understatement.

That's one of the not-so-fun things about being a professional hockey player. Everybody is all up in your business all the time, and there's a press release for everything.

Some days I really question my decision to shoot for pro hockey, but then I step out on the ice, and all the other bullshit I have to deal with fades away.

Hockey is my life. I live it, love it, and breathe it. All this other bullshit is worth it for those twenty minutes of ice time eighty-two nights a year.

Now I'm smashed between Lowell and Miller in the back seat of an Uber. Ryan and Harper are sitting in the seat in front of us, and Collin is in front, talking with the driver.

Lowell taps his legs against mine. He moves his eyes between Ryan and me.

"You good?"

I shrug. Am I good? I don't know.

"Of course he's good!" Miller says. "Dude just got hitched. Please tell me you're going to have a party to celebrate since it was so last minute and *none* of us were invited. Not that I'm going to hold that against you or anything."

A party? My first reaction is a big *Fuck no*.

But…a party might not actually be a bad idea. It would give Ryan and me a chance to introduce ourselves to everybody as a couple. Maybe it could help break the ice a little bit too.

"Actually," I say loud enough for Ryan to hear me, "I think a party would be a good idea. Don't you think so, *darling*?"

I swear I *hear* Ryan roll her eyes at the pet name. I picked up pretty quick that she is not a fan, and if she thinks I'm not going to keep using them just to fuck with her, she's wrong.

When she turns around, she has a big, fake-as-hell smile pasted on her face. "A party is a great idea, *honey*."

My lips twitch at the pet name she tosses back.

"Fuck yes!" Miller shouts. "Party time!"

How he's excited to party after a weekend in Vegas, I have no idea. I am all partied out. In fact, I could never party again and it would be too soon.

My phone vibrates in my pocket. I should probably ignore it, especially since I'm sure it's just my mom calling again, but I decide to check it anyway because I need the distraction. I can feel Lowell's gaze burning a hole in the side of my head. I know he wants to talk about everything, but I'm just not up for it right now.

Unknown: A party? Really??

It takes me a minute to catch on to who this could possibly be. Then the sad reality of it hits me—it's Ryan.

I don't even have my own wife's number saved on my phone.

I add it in and text her back.

. . .

Me: Trust me, I don't want to do this either, but I think it could help us. Get used to being seen together.

Me: It'll be good practice.

Ryan: Please tell me I'm not the only one who finds it incredibly sad that we have to practice being a couple.

It is sad. So very fucking sad.

Me: It's not just you.

Ryan: When are we having this party?

Me: I guess after you move in. Maybe an end-of-summer party?

Me: But I'm sure as soon as the press release goes out, everyone's going to be on our asses about it.

Ryan: PRESS RELEASE?! What for?

. . .

Ryan: Oh. Never mind. I forgot for a moment that you're famous.

Me: I'm not famous.

Ryan: Says the guy who randomly gets married in Vegas, then trends on Twitter about it.

Me: You're not exactly unknown yourself, Ms. 500k Followers.

Ryan: Why do I feel like you're making fun of me for having a social media presence?

Me: I'm not.

I'm really not making fun of her.

Do I understand it? No. But to be fair, all I do is play a game for a living and get beat up by other grown-ass men.

We both have weird careers when you think about it.

. . .

Me: I think what you do is kind of cool.

Me: But your photography is more my style.

Ryan: You've seen it?

Me: At Collin's place. It's nice.

She's only sitting a row in front of me, so I see the surprise cross her face. I'm not really sure how I feel about her being shocked that I complimented her.

I meant what I said. Her photography is nice. Actually, it's more than nice. It's pretty fucking incredible. The first time I went over to Collin's place and saw the three-piece set of the bridge we cross every day to go to the rink he has hanging over his fireplace, it took my breath away. Then he told me Ryan did it, and that shocked me even more. From all the shit Collin and Harper went through before, I knew she dabbled, but I didn't realize how talented she truly is.

I really want to ask her why she doesn't take it more seriously, but I don't feel like it's any of my business. Besides, I'm sure she has her reasons, and she doesn't owe me any sort of explanation.

. . .

Ryan: Thank you.

Me: You're welcome.

Ryan: Okay, stop being nice. It's weird.

Me: I take great offense to that.

Me: I'm plenty nice.

She actually laughs out loud at my response, and it pisses me off.

Me: Did you just laugh because I said I'm nice?

Ryan: You're not nice. You're grumpy.

Me: I thought I was hot and grumpy.

. . .

Ryan: Oh my god, you're not going to let me live that down, are you?

Me: Not a chance in hell.

Ryan: That's not very nice, husband.

Me: I thought you said I couldn't be nice, wife.

Ryan: You can be nice. Just not too nice. It's weird.

Me: Be nice but not too nice. Got it.

Ryan: You can add "Don't be annoying" to that list too.

Me: Now where's the fun in that?

Ryan: Are you finished being obnoxious?

Me: Nope, I'm just getting started.

. . .

Ryan: Wonderful.

Me: Just trying to keep your expectations of our marriage realistic, dear.

Ryan: You are just too good to me, sweetums.

That one makes me laugh out loud.

"Oh, gross. Are you two sexting right now?"

Lowell groans next to me, tossing his head back with exasperation. "Fuck's sake, Miller, shut up."

Then he mutters something about why the hell we invited the rookie to our weekend away.

He knows why. We wouldn't be on this celebration trip without him. Annoying as he is, we need Miller.

Luckily, the driver pulls up to the airport before we have to hear any more of Miller's bullshit.

Getting on our flight is quick and relatively painless. We only get stopped for autographs twice when a few people recognize us as we make our way to our gate.

I've grown so accustomed to flying on chartered jets that sometimes I forget what it's like to walk through an actual airport and be recognized. I don't typically do much traveling in the offseason. I tend to stay home and hibernate. If I do leave North Carolina, the only place I ever go is back home to upstate New York. Everyone there has known me since I was a little kid, so none of them are impressed by my career.

When I climb on board, I see Miller casually stowing his luggage in the bin directly above Ryan as if he's about to sit next to her. And because the kid apparently has balls the size of Texas, he does. He plops down like it's no big deal.

My brows slam together when he begins shuffling through his carry-on, talking a mile a minute because that's what Miller does. He doesn't notice that Ryan's not paying a lick of attention to anything he says.

She's too busy staring at me, the corners of her mouth tilted up into a smile.

She thinks this is funny.

But I doubt she'll find it funny when her new husband gets escorted off the plane for killing his teammate.

I step up in the aisle next to Miller and wait for him to realize I'm towering over him. It takes him far longer than I expect. When he does finally look up, his eyes are wide, and he realizes his mistake. It takes him .2 seconds to unclip his seat belt and shove to his feet.

"Uh, shit, my bad, Rhodes. I forgot you two were married for a second."

His cheeks are flaming red as he scuttles across the aisle to sit next to Lowell, who just shakes his head at him.

I settle into my seat and then turn to Ryan, sending her a big toothy grin. Now she's the one scowling as she turns away and focuses her attention out the window like she's loving the view even though we're still sitting on the tarmac.

The rest of the passengers file onto the plane, and after what feels like forever, we're finally on the move. The flight attendants begin going through their regular routine. I tune it out, having heard it a million times before.

"Before we take off today, we would like to welcome two very special guests to our flight," the perky voice says over the intercom.

Now *that* draws my attention, and warning bells start going off in my head. I glance over at Ryan, and she's sitting there with wide eyes too.

Oh fuck.

"Please join us in extending a huge congratulations to Ryan Bell and Stanley Cup champion Adrian Rhodes on their marriage. Let's give them a big round of applause."

Everyone starts clapping, and I want to die.

I want to just sink into my seat and pull my cap lower over my face when people start turning around to look at us.

Ryan's hand finds my thigh, and she digs her nails in deep. I look over to find her with another fake smile plastered across her face as she waves at everyone staring at us.

She's so good at faking that smile it makes me wonder

how often she practices.

"Smile," she mutters out of the corner of her mouth, not once dropping her grin.

"Huh?"

She digs her nails in deeper. "Smile, you idiot. Look happy."

Happy? The only thing that would make me happy right now is a stiff drink and for the earth to swallow me whole.

But we can't always get what we want.

So instead, I smile and wave, pretending to be blissfully in love right along with her.

"Why aren't they turning around?" she asks out of the corner of her mouth.

"No fucking clue, but I hate every second of this," I say back, my cheeks starting to hurt from smiling so much.

"Dude, kiss her! That's what they're waiting for!" Miller says, shoving at my shoulder from across the aisle.

A few loud whoops go around, and I realize that *is* what they're waiting for.

Because I don't think I can possibly take another second of everyone staring at me, I slide my palm up Ryan's face and drag her closer to me.

There's no mistaking the angry fire blazing in her eyes.

"Rhodes…" she warns quietly just before our lips touch.

I ignore the warning and press my lips to hers.

She inhales sharply when our mouths connect.

But, to my surprise, she doesn't pull away.

She kisses me back.

As drunk as I was, I remember our kiss at the altar. How soft and pliable her lips were. How sweet she tasted, even though the woman is full of fire.

But that drunken kiss? That drunken kiss was nothing compared to this.

Her lips are just as soft, and the taste of her is still sweet. But this time something feels different.

We feel different.

Her fingernails dig into my thigh again, but this time for an entirely different reason as she hums with pleasure. I slide my hand into her hair, pulling her closer, slanting my mouth over hers just so.

Just as I'm about to deepen the kiss, she pulls away without warning, stealing my breath as she goes.

She sucks in sharp breaths, eyes wide as she stares at me with surprise.

She doesn't have to tell me she felt it too. It's clear by the look on her face that she did. The plane erupts around us again, everyone enjoying the show.

Like the good actress that she is, she smiles and tucks a lock of hair behind her ear, blushing and hiding her face from the attention.

Finally, everyone goes back to minding their own business, turning around in their seats and ignoring us as they should have from the get-go.

But there's one stare I can't ignore.

I glance up and meet Collin's eyes. The look he's giving me…I don't know what it means, but I do know I don't like it.

Ignoring him, I turn my attention back forward, grabbing the magazine out of the back pocket of the seat in front of me and flipping mindlessly through the pages.

I have no idea how many minutes pass until Ryan speaks.

"What the hell was that?" she hisses quietly.

I turn to find her staring daggers at me.

"A kiss."

"I thought we said no kissing."

"No. We said no PDA and no sex. I know I'm a good kisser, but I didn't realize I was so good you mistook a kiss for sex."

If possible, her eyes narrow even more. "From here on out, no kissing."

"Afraid you might like it and want more?"

"No, I'm afraid I might vomit on you, and that won't look very good for us, now will it?"

I lean into her until my lips graze the shell of her ear. "Based on the way your nipples are poking through your shirt right now, I highly doubt that's something I need to be concerned with."

To her credit, she doesn't flinch or try to cover up when I call her out on it.

She gives me a saccharine smile. "Kiss me again and I'll knee you in the nuts."

I won't lie, said nuts retract into my body just a little

bit at the threat of harm.

"We're going to be together for a year, Ryan. We can't just *not* kiss. We're married. Married people kiss."

She squeezes her eyes shut. "I really wish you'd quit reminding me of that." She lets out a resigned sigh. "You're allowed a max of one kiss a week, but *only* if we're in a situation where it's warranted."

I lift a brow. "Just one? Please. I give it a week and you'll be begging me for more than that."

"In your dreams, Rhodes."

She pulls the hood of her jacket up over her head and leans against the window, burrowing into her seat as far away from me as possible and closing her eyes.

Of course she's a plane sleeper. I'm the exact opposite. I can never sleep on a plane.

"You know, now really isn't the time for a nap. We should be discussing the details of—"

She holds her hand up, cutting me off. "No. I need sleep to deal with you. Wake me up when we're a half hour from landing. We can talk then."

I want to argue with her, but much like her, I could use a bit of a break.

We're less than twenty-four hours into this marriage and I'm already tired. And if the dark circles under her eyes are any indicator, she's tired too.

"I can feel you staring at me, you know."

"Just admiring your beauty is all," I say with all the sarcasm I can muster.

She flips me off, and I laugh.

I fold my hands across my stomach and rest my head back against the seat. Even though I know I won't sleep, I close my eyes anyway.

I don't know how long it is before I hear a quiet, "Hey, Rhodes?"

"Hmm?" I respond, not opening my eyes.

"I'm sorry we're in this mess."

I sigh. "I'm sorry too."

I don't know why I do it, but I reach out and slide my hand over hers.

She doesn't pull away. Instead, she laces our fingers together, and I rub the ring on her finger.

And for the first time ever, I sleep on the flight home.

CHAPTER 9

RYAN

Rhodes kissed me.

Rhodes *really* kissed me.

And I kissed him back.

Like *really* kissed him back.

I knew what the people around us were waiting for, but I wasn't expecting Rhodes to give in to their silent request.

I really wasn't expecting him to slide his palm up my cheek and bring our lips together, nor was I ready for the charge that went through my body when our lips met. Even though it's on video, I barely remember our kiss at the altar, but something tells me no matter how good it was, there's no way it was as good as the kiss on the plane.

I don't fly too often, but when I do, I have a secret superpower that I can usually be asleep before takeoff. Yesterday, that was not the case.

Try as I might, I couldn't fall asleep with Rhodes

sitting right next to me, especially not after he kissed me the way he did.

So, I pretended to sleep while I held Rhodes' hand the whole flight.

As we left the airport, we didn't talk about it, and we're still not talking about it now as he drives me back to my apartment with that same damn scowl etched across his face, the air around us thick and full of unease.

It's like we have no idea what to say to each other.

If you ask me, it's ridiculous that I'm getting hung up on the fact that I kissed and held hands with my own husband, but here we are.

"I didn't realize you live so close to the arena," Rhodes says, breaking the silence. "The rent out here must be astronomical."

He has no idea.

I have a tiny one-bedroom, one-bathroom studio apartment, and I bet I pay at least half of what his mortgage payment is, plus I make a whole lot less than he does.

It used to not be so bad when I didn't have my grandmother's assisted living care to pay for, but now living here does make things pretty tight.

I've tried looking for a new place over the years, but nothing beats how close this is to my (former) job downtown and public transportation. If I were to move, I'd have to get a car, which would be a whole other expense to factor in, and I wouldn't be saving any money.

"This is me up here."

I point to an empty spot just up the street, and Rhodes expertly parks his SUV—which no doubt cost more than I've made in the last two years—then turns off the ignition.

I make a move to get out, not wanting to be trapped in this tension-filled vehicle any longer.

"Wait," Rhodes says, reaching out to stop me.

I try hard to ignore how warm his fingers feel wrapped around my wrist.

I turn toward him, brow arched. "Yeah?"

He doesn't say anything for a long moment. He just stares at me, and it's a stare that makes me uncomfortable. Like he's looking right down to the very parts of me I keep hidden.

I don't like it.

"When did you want to get your stuff moved to my place? I've got a pretty loaded schedule this week and want to get things sorted out."

"Oh. Um, I hadn't really thought about it. I guess tomorrow. Probably the sooner the better, right?"

He nods, then finally releases my wrist. I try not to think about how cold it makes me feel.

"Yeah, tomorrow is good. I can call some movers today, get some stuff set up."

"Movers? I don't think we'll be needing movers." I look around the fancy vehicle. "I'm pretty sure everything I own can fit in your SUV."

His brows rise. "Everything?"

"Yeah, probably. I don't really have that much. I'm a bit of a minimalist."

And broke, but he doesn't need to know that part.

"What about your bed? No way that will fit."

Bed? He has no clue that my "bed" consists of two mattresses stacked on top of each other in the corner of the room.

I've been frugal with my money over the last few years. Everything extra I get goes toward my grandmother's care and my student loans. Buying a new bed is very low on my list of things to do.

"We don't have to take that. You can buy me a new one."

He huffs out a laugh. "That so?"

I shrug. "We'll call it a wedding gift since I didn't get a real wedding."

He grimaces. "Do you want one? A real one?"

I've been planning my wedding since I was six years old when I used to make my Barbies get married all the time. I know the dress I want to wear, the flowers I want sprinkled everywhere, the centerpieces, the lighting, the music…I have it all planned, and it's nothing like the wedding I had.

Do I want a real wedding? Yes.

Just not with Rhodes.

"No."

He looks at me like he wants to press the issue, then thinks better of it. "All right. No wedding. Just a bed."

"A big bed. A sprawling bed. And a matching dresser."

Because right now, my clothes are hanging on wire racks.

"A whole new bedroom set—got it."

I sit back, satisfied with my requests. "Anything else, or am I free to go? My cat is waiting upstairs for me."

"You have a cat?"

"Is that a problem?"

"Does he like dogs?"

"*She* loves dogs."

"Good. Because I have one."

I don't know why, but this surprises me. I didn't really picture Rhodes having any pets at all. I always pictured him living alone in a dark and creepy castle on a hill.

"Well, I can't wait to meet her."

"*Him*," he mocks, and I narrow my eyes. "Tomorrow?"

"Tomorrow. I'll text you a time." He nods. "Can I go now?"

"What? No kiss for your husband?"

"I'll kiss your nuts with my knee."

He chuckles, but I see him not so subtly cover his junk.

I grab my bag from the back seat and hop out of the car, then climb the stairs to my apartment building. Just as I'm opening the front door, I hear his window roll down.

"Good night, my little sugar plum!"

With a groan, I slam the door closed.

I swear I hear him laugh.

Vivian Bell is a tiny woman, just shy of five foot two. She likely doesn't weigh an ounce over a hundred and twenty-five pounds, and she's 78 years young.

She's my grandmother, and she's the most important person in my life.

"Hey, Grams," I say as I wrap my arms around her small frame the best I can as she sits in her favorite chair in the rec center of the facility. As usual, she has a word search book spread out in front of her. She's obsessed with the damn things, going through a book a month on average.

She hugs me back. "Where you been, kid? I missed you for dinner last night."

A frown tugs at my lips. "I was in Vegas, remember?"

"Oh, yes. I remember now. You took that strapping young man with you, right?"

I laugh because she can't remember that I was in Vegas, but she sure as hell remembers Collin.

After fighting with her management for two weeks to get a new bookshelf up in her room, I finally gave in and asked Collin if he could come over and help put it together for her. He was more than happy to oblige, and to say my grandmother fell in love with him would be an understatement.

She recently became a hockey fan thanks to the other residents here getting her into it during the Comets Cup run, and when star defenseman Collin Wright walked through her door, she was over the moon…and immediately started in on him about his stats.

He took it all in stride and promised to come back again another time with Harper. They now stop by once a month to spend a few hours with my grandmother, who Harper has always been close with too.

"How was the trip? You didn't get into too much trouble, did you?"

A pit forms at the bottom of my stomach at her words.

Too much trouble? Try *all* the trouble.

"Actually, Grams, that's what I'm here to talk to you about today."

"Oh no, my little Beauty. I know that tone. What happened?"

I grin at her nickname for me.

When I was younger, I was obsessed with *Beauty and the Beast*. Mostly because I really wanted the sweet library like Belle had, but still. We're talking *watching it every day*, *practically living in my replica Belle dress*, and *talking to the dishes* kind of obsessed.

Because of that, my grandmother began to call me Beauty.

Fitting now, especially since I'm married to The Beast.

Speaking of…

I take a steadying breath. "Well, there's this guy I've been seeing for a while." Not a complete lie. I have known Rhodes for a while. "Things…well…they got very serious very fast. And we sort of…got married."

She lifts a brow, eyeing me stoically. "Sort of?"

"Well, we did. W-We got…married. We're married." The word keeps tripping me up, and I pray she doesn't see through my facade.

She continues to stare at me, and finally, after what feels like twenty excruciating minutes, a big smile breaks out across her face, and she claps her hands together. "Oh, I am so happy for you, dear!" She gasps. "It's not to that Steven fella, is it?"

"No. We broke up, remember?"

Her shoulders sag in relief. "Good. I never liked that little asshole."

I bark out a laugh. My grandma might be old and petite and have to use a walker to get around most days, but she's full of fire where it counts.

"Well, who is he? Tell me all about him."

"Wait…you're happy?"

"Of course I'm happy. Whatever makes you happy makes me happy, and you got that glow about you, so I have nothing to worry about."

"But you don't think it was too sudden or anything?"

"Pffft!" She waves her hand at me. "When you know, you know, right, dear?"

I can't help but think of Rhodes saying the same thing.

The romantic in me wants to agree, but this isn't romantic. There's nothing romantic about any of this at all.

I should have known Grams would think otherwise though. After all, she's the one who introduced me to romantic comedies and romance novels and taught me the real meaning of love.

"Tell me everything about him. When do I get to meet this fine young man who has swept my little Beauty off her feet?"

I hadn't really thought that far ahead. I guess Rhodes does need to meet my grandmother. After all, he will be the one paying for her care for the next year.

"Well, he has a pretty busy schedule, so I'll have to get with him and find a time where he can come and get to know you some. I guess you kind of technically already know him."

Her gray brows furrow. "I do?"

I nod. "Well, he, uh, he works with Collin."

Her green eyes—the same shade as mine—grow in size. "You've married a hockey player?"

I nod again. "Yep. I…married a hockey player."

"Ooh, girl." She licks her lips. "You could bounce a quarter off their asses."

"Grams!"

She lifts her dainty shoulder. "What? Just because I'm old doesn't mean I can't appreciate the nice things in life anymore."

I shake my head, grinning.

She's not wrong about that. Hockey players *do* have some nice butts, and Rhodes is no exception to this rule.

"Is that how you two met? Through Harper?"

"Yeah, I guess you could say that." Ugh, we really need to get our story straight. "We've been dancing around one another for months." Not totally untrue. Any time I've tried to befriend Rhodes, he's always walked away from me. "You know how it can be on vacation. Sometimes those feelings you keep bottled up can just come right out, and that's what happened. We just looked at each other and knew."

Bullshit, bullshit, bullshit. All of it lies.

"Awww." She places her hand over her heart. "That is just too sweet. How did he propose?"

I don't remember it.

I was up half the night last night trying to remember any details of our wedding beyond what was posted online. I remember the diner and him forcing me to eat to sober me up some. I remember the look on his face when he learned the woman he loves is marrying someone else. And I remember him begging me to help him forget.

But after that, it's pretty blank.

"He put the ring in a glass of champagne."

She frowns. "A little unoriginal, but show me the ring and we'll see if he can redeem himself."

The ring? Fuck!

"It's, uh, getting resized."

Another lie. The ring fits fine. I just took it off this morning because I couldn't stand the sight of it. I made the mistake of getting on my phone and saw all the notifications I had. There were a few comments about how it had to be fake, and I even saw an article saying the same thing.

Just looking at the ring knowing they were right made my stomach hurt, so I took it off.

"Oh, well, that's too bad. Hopefully it'll be ready next time when you come to visit."

"I'm sure it will be. Speaking of visiting, I have some good news."

She perks up at my announcement. "More good news?"

Oh, right. I forgot my marriage was supposed to be good news too.

"Yes." I lean in closer. "Don't say anything just yet, but we're going to be moving you out of here and into a new place soon."

I'm not quite sure what I thought she'd do, maybe jump out of her chair, do a little dance. I definitely wasn't expecting her lips to pull down in a frown.

"Oh, Beauty, as much as I appreciate that, I know this place is already a bit out of budget."

I don't talk to my grandmother about how much this facility costs, but I shouldn't be surprised that of course she knows.

"It's fine, Grams. My…husband wants to do this for you."

"Does he really?"

I nod. "Yes. He knows you mean the world to me, and he wants to take good care of you."

Her shoulders sink with relief. "Oh, gosh. I am so happy to hear that. You found yourself a good one. You make sure you keep him."

If she only knew…

Grams steers the conversation toward all the drama happening around the facility. Her roommate, Deana, had a friend over, and after a few too many bottles of wine, a male stripper showed up at Grams' door and… well, let's just say that friend is no longer permitted on the premises.

We chat for a while longer, and I tell her about Harper's good news she shared with me this morning—she and Collin are moving in together. Grams looks a little heartbroken that Collin won't be leaving Harper for her anytime soon, but she tells me to pass on her congratulations anyway.

My phone buzzes in my pocket and I pull it out to check it.

Rhodes: I'm here.

. . .

Oh, shit. I completely forgot Rhodes was meeting me at my apartment to help me move.

My landlord wasn't too happy with my last-minute move-out when I called this morning, but I don't really care. It's not like he hasn't left me high and dry plenty of times in the years I've lived there.

Rhodes: Where are you???

Me: Hold your horses. I'll be there in a bit.

Three dots appear on the screen. Bounce, bounce, bounce they go. Then they disappear.

Appear, disappear.

Something tells me he is not pleased right now.

Me: I can feel you glaring at me through the phone.

Me: I'm with my grandmother. Time got away from me.

. . .

Rhodes: You're with your grandma? Don't you think I should have come with you? Met her?

He's probably right. He should be here to meet her for many different reasons.

But I wanted to tell Grams about Rhodes on my own. You know, just in case the crazy old bat flew out of her chair and maimed him for marrying her granddaughter on a whim in Vegas. Then I'd have to bail her out of jail, and it would be a whole thing—one I don't have the time or patience to deal with right now.

Rhodes: I mean, I AM going to be paying her bills.

Me: I mean, I AM helping you fake a marriage.

Rhodes: Point taken.

Rhodes: Just hurry up. I'm starving and want to get this shit done.

"Now, dear, who has you frowning like that? I hope it's not your new man."

I tuck my phone back into my pocket, turning my attention to a worried-looking Grams. "It's nothing I can't handle."

She chucks my chin. "Attagirl. Tough, just like I taught you."

And she did. Harper always calls me Ryan the Lion, but she has no idea that I'm a cute cub compared to Grams.

"Listen, Grams, I gotta jet."

"Got some ass to whoop?" She sticks her little fists up, punching at a pretend victim.

Man, I love this woman. She's tough on the outside, sweet on the inside.

"That's right." I wink at her, then wrap her in another hug. "I'll be back on Sunday for our usual dinner, okay?"

She crooks her finger at me, beckoning me closer. "Bring burgers. It's meatloaf this weekend, and it tastes like cat turds."

"You got it," I whisper conspiratorially.

Every Sunday I stop by to have dinner with her and bring her something different for dinner. I figure it's the least I can do since she's stuck in this crummy place.

But not for much longer. Soon, she'll be out of here and on to somewhere much better.

I just have to keep reminding myself that all this crap with Rhodes is worth it because Grams will be happy.

That's all that matters.

My phone buzzes again.

. . .

Rhodes: A "Yes, husband" would be nice.

I grit my teeth, pocketing my phone.

I give Grams one last kiss, then head out.

For Grams, I remind myself as I leave to definitely *not* murder my husband.

CHAPTER 10

RHODES

Ryan: You are so annoying.

Ryan: I'm on my way. Happy now?

Me: Thrilled.

Me: Now stop texting and driving.

Ryan: Yes, husband. *eye roll emoji*

I laugh, tossing my phone into the passenger seat.

I lean back, resting my head against the headrest, and close my eyes since apparently Ryan is going to be a while still.

For someone who travels a lot for work, you would think I'd have it down pat, but it always seems to take a lot out of me. Add in having to talk with my mom—that's an hour's worth of ass chewing—an early-morning shift at the summer hockey camp the Comets run down at the rink, and then a meeting with my general manager and coach, which was a whole other level of exhausting, and I'm fucking beat.

That's not even including the debacle from this weekend and my lack of sleep from dealing with everything.

I really hope getting Ryan settled in goes quickly. I need a nap pronto.

My ringtone chimes over the car speakers. I peek at the infotainment screen and see it's Brittney calling. She's been doing this a lot lately. So often in fact that my inbox is full of messages from her that I refuse to listen to. I should probably delete them.

I ignore the call, and just as I close my eyes, my phone goes off again. This time it's an incoming call from a number I don't recognize.

"No, thanks, spam caller."

I press the end button and lean my head back again.

Not even ten seconds later, my phone rings again.

Okay, this is just annoying.

I hit the answer button without looking at the screen and let out a growly, "What."

"Well, I hope that's not how you answer the phone when your wife calls."

Shit.

"Sorry, my bad, Shep. What's up?"

"What's up? *What's up?* That's the best you've got for me?" He laughs derisively. "You get married over the weekend and don't give your agent any sort of heads-up about it, and then when he finally gets ahold of you, your response is *What's up?*"

He has me there.

"Uh, my bad."

"I think that's even worse." He laughs. "So, are you going to tell me what the hell happened?"

I sigh, scrubbing a hand over my face. "I don't even know where to start."

"Well, I'm going to go ahead and take a guess that this marriage wasn't at all planned and there might have been a little bit of alcohol involved."

Now it's my turn to laugh. "That obvious, huh?"

"Nah. I've just been there before. I got married in Vegas myself. We had Elvis do our vows."

"You were married before Denver?"

"Nope. That's who I married. Granted, we were already in a committed relationship, which I'm guessing is a lot more than I can say for you."

I'm mildly annoyed by how well he knows me, but I guess that's to be expected when you've been working with the same person for as many years as I've been with Shep.

Shepard Clark, former pro baseball star and World

Series champion, has been my agent since I finally made it to the big leagues. Collin signed with him first, and after hearing his raving recommendation, I decided to give him a shot too. And boy, am I glad I did. I don't think there are many agents out there who wouldn't be blowing up their players' phones if they got married without telling them. But Shep has only dropped me a single text asking me to call when I'm ready. He's more the type of guy to sit back and let us come to him if we need him. That might not be a good style for a lot of players, but I like his approach. I like that I can still be a grown-ass adult and not feel like I have a babysitter but also know I have somebody there who has my back when I need it.

"I had no idea you and Denver got married in Vegas."

"Yeah, it was kind of a last-minute thing. She was pregnant, but she lost the baby shortly after. I mean, not that I married her because she was pregnant. I was head over heels in love with the woman, but...I'm rambling. You know what I mean though."

I don't know. I don't know what he means because Ryan and I were not in love.

We were just drunk.

"You would be correct to assume there was a lot of alcohol involved," I tell him.

"This have anything to do with your ex getting engaged to that dickhead former teammate of yours?"

"It...was a factor. Definitely led me to drinking. Not

sure what led me to the altar though. Not really my finest moment."

"No, I'd say not. So, this wife of yours—that's Harper's friend Ryan, yeah?"

"Yeah, that's her. Do you know her?"

"Sort of. Denver is friends with her. We have a couple of her photographs hanging up around our house. She's talented as hell."

Agreed.

"Anyway," Shep says, "I guess the real reason I'm calling is…do I need to be worried about this last-minute marriage?"

What he's really asking is: Is this going to fuck up my season?

"No. We have it under control."

"Do I even want to know the details?"

"Probably not. But it's fine. I promise."

"Okay. Comets know it's all a sham?"

I chuckle. Leave it to Shep to call it what it is. He's a straight shooter, and that's what I like about him.

Do the Comets know it's a sham? No.

I told them I've been seeing Ryan for a while now and things were getting serious, so we decided to elope, and they took it at face value. I think a lot of that has to do with the fact that I'm not known as a guy who makes rash decisions. I'm the thinker. The levelheaded one. The guy who makes calculated choices. I'm fairly sure that played into them believing this wasn't just some spur-of-the-moment thing.

Did I still get my ass reamed for making headlines? Fuck yes.

But I think if I keep my nose down this upcoming season, it'll all blow over. The new public relations rep who joined the organization last summer agreed with me on that too.

Truthfully, they were more concerned about how Brittney being engaged to Colter is going to affect my performance on the ice when we play Florida.

I told them it wouldn't, and I plan to keep that promise.

Colter isn't worth my time, and neither is Brittney. What's done is done. I have bigger fish to fry, like convincing the world I'm in love with my wife.

"What sham? This is real. I am *super* in love."

He laughs again. "From a PR standpoint, good answer. As a friend…good luck with that?" I hear a commotion on the other end of the line, and a kid starts to cry in the background. "Oh, fuck. I gotta go, man. Do yourself a favor—never have children."

Every time I talk to him, he feeds me the same line, but I know he loves his kids.

"Listen," he says, "if you need anything, just call. If there's a shitstorm, we'll work through it. Just maybe give me a heads-up next time, yeah?"

"I can do that. And, Shep? Thanks for being so chill about this."

"Man, if you only knew half the stupid shit I did in my day…" He huffs out a laugh. "We all make mistakes.

It's just how we choose to deal with them that matters. But know if shit hits the fan with this one, I am married to a journalist, and we'll help spin the story however you'd like, okay?"

"Appreciate it."

There's another loud commotion. "Fucking hell. Duty calls, man. Talk later."

"Later."

The call disconnects just as Ryan rounds the corner.

It's midafternoon and the sun is hanging high in the sky right behind her. From this angle, it almost looks like she's wearing a halo.

But I know the truth. That's no halo—those are horns.

She's full of too much sass for it to be a halo.

I hop out of the car and meet her just as she begins walking up the steps to her apartment. She doesn't greet me; she just gives me side-eye.

I smirk at her. "Hi, *wife*."

"*Husband*," she retorts with disdain, narrowing her eyes at me. "Ready to get packing?"

"Packing? You haven't packed yet?"

"Nope," she says, popping the P as she pushes her key into the lock. "I've been busy."

"Busy? Doing what?"

"Washing my hair." She tosses the quip over her shoulder as we begin climbing the stairs.

I'm not dumb. I know that's the go-to girl answer when they don't want to do something.

I pinch a lock of blonde hair between my fingertips. "If that's the case, you didn't do a very good job. It's looking a bit *dull*."

She gasps, whirling around to smack at me. "You ass!"

"Right back at you, babe. You should have thought about that before you decided to skip out on packing your shit up so we could make this move a lot faster."

"Excuse me if I'm not very excited to pack up my entire life and move in with you." She turns back around, stomping up the stairs double time.

The only problem is I have almost a foot on her and keep up with her with zero issues.

She doesn't like this either.

By the time we reach her door, she's pissed and literally shuts it in my face, leaving me out in the hall.

I sigh, hanging my head, cursing drunk me for what feels like the millionth time for getting into this mess.

I push open her door and am instantly greeted by an adorable black fluffball darting out into the hallway.

"Poe!"

Ryan takes off after her, brushing past me with a glare. She catches the cat just before she darts down the stairs. She walks back to the apartment, snuggling her up to her chest. As she passes me, I hear her whisper into the cat's ear about what a little brat she is.

"Gotta be careful with the doors. She loves to run out of them," Ryan says, setting the cat down only once I've closed the door.

The cat eyes me from across the room, and I notice that her eyes are the same shade as her owner's. She takes small, tentative steps toward me, and I crouch down to meet her on her level, holding my hand out so she can get a sniff.

The tip of her nose is chilly as she brushes against my fingers a few times. She must decide I'm pretty okay, because the next thing I know, she's dropping her weight in the palm of my hand.

"Yeah, she does that. It means she wants you to hold her," Ryan says from the kitchen where she's pulling things from the cabinets. And by from the kitchen, I mean directly to my right, because really, this whole place is one big room.

And it's a tiny room at that. I think my garage is bigger than the whole apartment…and I don't have that big of a garage.

I look around the open area. Ryan wasn't kidding when she said there wasn't much she has to take with her. The place is sparsely decorated, and there's no big furniture. I'm trying hard not to concentrate on the cheap mattresses stacked on top of one another in the corner.

No wonder she wants a new bed.

There's a small vanity set up in the corner and a ring light beside it.

"Is that where you make your videos?"

"Yep."

She doesn't elaborate, but something in her quick response has me asking…

"Do you like it?"

She pauses in her packing, looking at me. "Huh?"

"Doing the influencer thing…do you like it?"

Her nose scrunches up, and it's kind of cute. "I hate that word. *Influencer.* It sounds so…superficial." I agree. "But, yeah, it's fun."

"Would you rather be doing something else though?"

She considers the question a moment. "Yes and no. I love the creativity of it, but I hate the social media aspect of it. Photography is another big passion of mine, and I'd honestly like to do more with that other than take selfies of my makeup."

"You do some drop-in exhibits downtown, yeah?"

She seems surprised I know. "Uh, yeah. Sometimes. I like doing interactive ones, and they usually seem to be a hit."

"The one you did with Harper and Collin…that was kind of rough. I saw some of those photographs. They were very…raw."

"What can I say? I like it rough and raw." Her eyes widen when she realizes how that sounds. "Emotionally. I meant emotionally. As in I like to capture the raw human emotion."

I hold back my laugh. "Noted."

"Anyway, enough about me." She waves her hand. "Did you talk to your boss people?"

"My boss people?" I grin. "Yeah, I spoke with the GM and my coaches."

"And? What'd you tell them?"

"The truth." Her mouth slackens. "That you're madly in love with me and you couldn't wait to marry me, so you got me drunk and made me do it in Vegas."

She rolls her eyes. "Sounds wildly accurate. I'm sure they bought it."

"Actually, they did."

"Really?"

I nod. "Yep. They wrote up a quick press release just to get the media who is questioning it off our backs. It'll go out tonight."

I fucking loathe the media. It's my least favorite thing about playing hockey. I avoid headlines at all costs and rarely do any after-game press. Sometimes I'll have a quick chat with our home announcer, but that's it. I'm not standing around while a bunch of people shove cameras and mics in my face.

"Wow. That is…wow." She shakes her head. "So, uh, I guess this is all real, then, huh?"

"Afraid so." The cat snuggles into me, wanting my attention, so I scratch her ears. She purrs against me. "You said her name is Poe?"

"Yep."

"Like Edgar Allan Poe?"

"No, like Poe Dameron. Because she's a badass just like him."

I grin. Ryan has a nerd side. Huh. Who knew?

"She's sweet." I continue scratching between her ears, and she pushes her head into my hand.

Ryan snorts. "She likes to pretend she's sweet. Really, she's just a spoiled brat who is a total bitch if she doesn't get her way."

"How old is she?"

"About six months. I actually adopted her from that animal shelter Harper and Collin are always volunteering at."

"Really? That's where I got my dog too."

"Those damn do-gooders rubbing off on us. I swore I'd never get a pet, but one look at Poe and I was a goner. She had me wrapped around her finger like you are now. Until—"

"Ow! Motherfucker!" Poe sinks her teeth into my finger, and I swear she grins up at me around it.

"That. Until that."

I pull my finger from Poe's mouth, and she jumps from my arms, strutting away like she hasn't a care in the world.

Ryan pads into the living room and grabs my finger, inspecting it.

"I'm sorry. She's difficult sometimes. I think she's just still adjusting to…well, being alive. She's like a toddler. Totally unpredictable," she explains, tugging me back into the kitchen.

I let her lead me to a tiny, café-style table. She shoves me down in the chair, then spins around and reaches over the top of the fridge, standing on her tiptoes to get to the cabinet above it. She struggles a moment to reach whatever she's looking for but then spins back around with the first aid kit in hand.

I want to laugh at her because a kitten bite is nothing compared to the injuries I'm used to. I get hit by two-hundred-plus-pound adults skating over 15 MPH and take slapshots from pucks soaring six times that. This isn't shit compared to that.

But she seems determined to care for me, so…I let her.

And I don't know why I let her.

I think it's because of the way she traps the tip of her tongue between her teeth as she concentrates on squeezing just a miniscule amount of antibiotic ointment out of the tube and rubbing it gently on the two puncture wounds. The way a little crinkle of skin forms between her eyebrows as she opens the bandage and peels back the protective layers. The way all of her attention is focused on getting the Band-Aid to sit just right on my finger.

There's no denying that Ryan is an attractive woman. Her hair is that peculiar shade of blonde that has all kinds of tones mixed in when you look close enough. Her eyes are the most unique shade I've ever seen, a deep dark forest hue around the outer edges that lightens up around the iris. Her nose is just on this side of too small for her face, but the way it turns up at the end is too fucking cute. And there's a little beauty mark just under her right eye.

She looks like a more natural, modern-day, green-eyed Marilyn Monroe—beautiful with that edge to her that makes you just slightly tremble in her presence, but in the best way possible.

"I can feel you staring at me," she says quietly as she tucks the supplies back in the kit.

It's on the tip of my tongue to apologize, but why should I apologize? She's my wife; I can stare at her if I want.

She picks up the first aid kit to put it back in the cabinet above the refrigerator. Just like she struggled to get it down, she battles to toss it back up there. Her lean body stretches out long as she presses up on the tips of her toes once again. Her ass pushes out toward me, and my god is it a beautiful ass.

Before I know it, I've risen from the table and I'm standing behind her. Her breath hitches when I press against her, and she halts all movement.

I don't know what I'm doing, but I can't *not* be next to her right now.

I place my hands on her hips, unable to stop myself from touching her. She takes another stuttered breath, and I swear I can feel her heart beating.

My fingers dig into her waist as I breathe her in. She smells so good standing this close, like sunshine and fresh lemons and just a hint of something else. It's the same way she smelled at the club when we were dancing, and it's making me feel the same way it did then too.

She swallows thickly, and I can feel her trembling

beneath my touch as I slip my fingers under the hem of her shirt. Her skin is soft, and I bet it tastes as good as it smells.

I lean forward, brushing my lips against the exposed skin on her neck. I brush my lips back and forth and back again, pressing soft kisses everywhere I can.

This is exactly what I pictured this morning as I palmed my cock in the shower—her body beneath my lips.

She makes a low sound in her throat, and it's enough to pull me from whatever daze I'm in.

What the fuck are you doing, Rhodes? Quit touching her. She's not really yours to touch.

With reluctance, I step away from her, putting distance between us once again, and I hear her exhale a shaky breath.

"We should pack that," I say, hoping she doesn't notice how scratchy my voice is right now or call me out on what just happened.

"Right. Packing." She clears her throat and sets the first aid kit on the counter beside her. She runs a hand through her hair, then turns to me.

I wait for it. Wait for her to yell at me for putting my hands on her. For kissing her.

But she doesn't.

All she says is, "Ready to get started?"

CHAPTER 11

RYAN

Just like that, my whole life is turned upside down.

Okay, fine. My life was turned upside down several days ago, but moving out of the first apartment I've ever had is definitely a big deal.

I glance around my new bedroom and am shocked by the amount of space I have in here. My old apartment was one giant room, and by giant, I mean very tiny. This new bedroom is half the size of what my whole apartment was.

I think people are under the impression that I have this glamorous life because people follow me on social media, but that's not the case at all. I'm struggling just like everybody else.

The fact that the entirety of my possessions can fit into the back of just one SUV proves that.

Even though I didn't have a lot to move, I am still somehow exhausted when we carry in the last box. I think it's all the drama of the last few days finally catching up to me.

"Hey."

Rhodes startles me, appearing in my bedroom door out of nowhere with his adorable one-year-old Cavalier King Charles Spaniel, Frodo, in his arms.

"Sorry," he mutters.

"It's fine."

We didn't talk much as we packed my apartment. You could even say we went as far as to completely ignore one another, which was a difficult feat in such a tiny space. But it was awkward after he did…well, whatever you want to call what he did.

I try to shake off how he felt pressed against me. Big and warm and just right.

And I really don't want to think about the way his lips felt ghosting against my neck.

"I'm starving," he says, interrupting my thoughts before I do something really dumb like moan. "Do you want to order something for dinner?"

My stomach rumbles at the mention of food, but my first reaction is to say no, I can't afford it.

Before I can get the words out, Rhodes says, "My treat."

I am not about to argue with that.

"Sure, what did you have in mind?"

"Doesn't matter to me. I'm not picky. Whatever you'll eat, I'm fine with."

"Hmm, too much against your diet if I wanted to order stuffed crust meat lover's pizza?"

"I think I can survive one stuffed crust pizza, but only

if we can add extra green peppers."

"And breadsticks. Maybe wings too?"

"Fuck it, why don't we throw in dessert too?"

"Really?"

"No. Just pizza. I'll order it and take Frodo out for a walk while you finish settling in. There's a really good place that delivers here."

"I'll let Poe out for a bit to explore while you're gone, if that's okay?"

"Sounds good," he says, but he doesn't make a move to leave.

"Yes?" I ask.

He runs a hand over his jaw. "I noticed you aren't wearing your ring."

Oh.

"I, uh, I took it off for moving," I lie, my heart racing in my chest.

He tilts his head, his hazel eyes boring into me. If he knows I'm lying, he doesn't say anything.

Instead, he nods again. "Okay. But, Ryan?"

"Yes?"

"I'd like you to wear it."

The way he says it…I don't know. It's almost like he's hurt that I don't have it on, and I didn't expect him to care, honestly.

"Okay. I'll wear it," I promise. And I mean it. I'll slip it back on tonight.

"Okay."

This time he does walk away, leaving me to finish

unpacking.

I give myself a shake, pushing away the ring conversation because I do not have the brain power to overthink it right now, and start on unboxing all of my clothes. I felt very smart when I decided to leave them all on the hangers, making this part super easy.

It's not that I ever lived a lavish lifestyle before, but after my grandmother took a fall and needed to go into the facility, I really started to take a look at my budget. One thing I realized was that I spent entirely too much money on clothes I didn't wear. So, I sold a bunch of pieces online to make some cash, then went shopping for a capsule wardrobe. Now I just rotate the same thirty or so pieces. Seeing everything lined up in this massive closet makes me want to laugh, and maybe cry a little because it's becoming increasingly clear that I do not belong here.

I'm just Ryan Bell, the girl whose parents abandoned their children to travel the country in an RV. The girl who was raised by her grandparents, went to public school, and had to take out so much money in student loans to get a BFA she doesn't even use.

I love that my grandparents were so encouraging and always pushed us to follow our dreams, to get a degree in something that interested us, something we were passionate about.

But when my grandfather passed away unexpectedly and shit hit the fan financially for them and then my grandmother had her fall, I quickly realized I made a huge mistake. I didn't need a degree in something that excited me. I needed a degree in something practical. And now I'm paying the price, married to a guy I don't even love just to pay my bills.

What a fucking life.

I continue unpacking my room until Rhodes calls out to tell me the pizza is here.

"Finally. I am starving," I say as I make my way into the kitchen, which is also massive.

He gave me a quick tour earlier, but I really didn't pay much attention to just how wide and open everything is. It's totally blowing my mind.

Rhodes grabs two plates from the cabinet next to the giant stainless steel fridge, and I make a mental note that that's where the dishes are kept. He sets them on the counter as I slide onto the barstool tucked under the ledge.

"Drink?" he asks, heading for the fridge.

"Water is fine."

It's not fine. I actually hate water, but I don't want to be a burden right now.

When I feel him staring at me, I look up. "What?"

"Do you really want water or do you want something else?"

"Actually, if you have some milk, that would be nice."

He wrinkles his nose. "Milk?"

I shrug. "What? It's good with pizza."

"Whatever you say."

He reaches into the fridge and pulls out a fancy glass

carafe full of milk. Who actually puts milk in a glass carafe? Why is he not drinking it straight from the carton like a normal person?

He grabs a cup from the cabinet next to the plates, pours me a generous glass, then slides it my way. He leaves the carafe on the counter just in case I want more.

I notice there's more than one box sitting on the counter.

He lied.

He totally got breadsticks and dessert.

He pulls open the lid of the pizza box and nods toward dinner. "Dig in."

And we do.

I'm halfway through my third slice and second breadstick when I just can't take any more. I toss the half-uneaten pizza onto the plate and lean back on my stool, resting my hand on my stomach.

"Ugh. I can't. I can't do any more."

"Wuss." Rhodes snatches my pizza off my plate and shoves the rest of it into his mouth in one bite.

I'm a little impressed, but I don't say that. "Didn't your mom teach you any manners?"

"Yes. So don't tell her I did that when you meet her."

I think about that…the fact that I'm going to have to meet Rhodes' parents and pretend to be married to him in front of them.

"What are they like?"

"My parents?" I nod. "I don't know…parents."

"Yeah, but what's that like? Not all of us had parents."

A frown tugs at his lips, and I don't like the sympathy I see in his eyes. Thankfully, he doesn't ask any questions and moves on.

"Their names are Margaret and Oscar, but my mom goes by Maggie. They've been married for thirty years, and they are the epitome of a perfect marriage."

I raise my brow. "A perfect marriage? Those don't exist."

Not even my grandparents had a perfect marriage, but that's what I loved about them. They had dark spots, but they always worked through them. To me, that's the real definition of a solid relationship. Not one that doesn't have its problems—just one that doesn't let the problems win.

That's what I want.

"As close to perfect as you can get, trust me."

"When are your parents coming to visit next?"

"They'll be here for my first home game. It's tradition. So, we'll have some time to practice being married before then."

Practice being married.

I like how he just glazes right over that like it's not a completely fucked-up phrase to use.

"What about your brother? Is he coming to visit soon?"

"Ha. I wish. But no. He was really close with my grandfather and he passed… Well, he hasn't really been back to the States that often. He's definitely that guy who is married to his career."

"I can understand that. I've been married to hockey since I was a teen. But he should be helping you, you know."

I don't disagree with him because he's right. My brother *should* be helping me, and I'm sure he would if he actually knew how hard things have become. But I don't want to burden him with it. Besides, it's not like I was on the verge of being homeless or anything. I (mostly) had it managed even without the help from Rhodes. Now I can just breathe a little easier.

Well, as good as one can breathe being married to someone they don't love.

Rhodes clears his throat and sits back, tossing his balled-up napkin onto his plate.

"So, I take it you're too full for dessert, then?"

I perk up. "Dessert?"

"Yeah, it looks like some brownies made it into my cart when I was checking out."

Made it into his cart, huh? He totally bought me dessert, and for some reason, that really warms my heart.

"I wonder how that happened."

"No clue, but since they're here, we might as well eat them, right?"

"Brownies sound so good, but I'm seriously full right now. Rain check?"

"Rain check it is."

"All I want at the moment is a shower and to sleep for

like eight to nine hours." I gasp. "Oh, shit! A bed! I don't have a bed to sleep in."

"Ah, fuck. In my dire state of hunger, I kind of forgot we needed to go shopping. I'm sure everywhere is closed by now."

"Where the hell am I going to sleep tonight?"

"You can sleep in my bed."

I balk at his suggestion. "I'm not sleeping with you, Rhodes. I thought we covered this."

"I'm going to pretend I didn't just hear the utter disgust in your voice, and I was not referring to sleeping with me. I just said you could sleep in my bed."

"Where will you sleep?"

"I'll take the couch." He shrugs. "I don't know if you've sat on that thing yet, but it's comfortable as fuck. I take all my pre-home-game naps there."

An image of Rhodes snuggled on the couch before a game races across my mind. What I'm not expecting is for the image to transform and for me to be wrapped in his arms.

I shake the thought away. "I don't want to put you out."

Rhodes puts his hand to his chest. "Did you just display an emotion other than complete displeasure for me?"

I barely resist the urge to roll my eyes. "Yeah, but don't get used to it."

"Ah, there she is." He shakes his head. "You can take my bed tonight, and tomorrow after I get done with practice, we can go furniture shopping. Apparently, I owe you a new bedroom set."

"You have practice tomorrow?"

"*I* don't have practice tomorrow, but I have to help with practice."

I tilt my head, not understanding.

"I volunteer during the summer to help out the Comets junior league."

He volunteers? And with children? That…surprises me. He's always so…well, Rhodes. Grumpy and always looking half annoyed. I'm surprised he works with children.

"Before you start getting ideas like me being nice, just know it's practically mandatory."

"And here I thought you might have a heart in there somewhere under all those cantankerous scowls."

"Cantankerous? Oh. Nice eighteen-point word."

"You *Scrabble*?"

"I dabble."

This time I do roll my eyes at him, pushing away from the counter. "And on that note, I'm done for the night."

I hop down from my stool and gather my plate, deposit it into the dishwasher. I clean up our mess, condense the number of boxes down, and put them in the fridge along with the milk Rhodes left out for me.

That tension that seems to permanently exist between us slowly fills the air. It's like this every time we're in the same room for more than a few minutes.

It's suffocating, and I need an escape.

"Do you mind if I take a shower?"

"Not at all. This is your house too. You don't have to ask to shower."

I…I hadn't thought of that. This *is* my home, isn't it? At least for the next year.

"Thanks," I murmur, making my way back down the hall to my bedroom.

I gather up my shower items and pajamas—I really don't need to be caught by Rhodes in nothing but a towel—and then head into the guest bathroom.

I'm not at all surprised to find that even the bathroom is gigantic. There's a huge tub to one side and a walk-in shower…in the *guest bathroom.*

The tub calls my name because I love a good bath, but I think a shower is what I need tonight. I'll test the bath out later.

For a brief moment, I wonder how much money Rhodes actually makes. Apparently, it's enough to afford a place like this, spend random weekends in Vegas in swanky hotel suites, and drop thousands of dollars a month on my grandmother's care.

I strip out of my clothes, feeling all gross and sticky from moving, and step into the shower.

I crank the water up to full blast, and I'm not even a little bit ashamed of the moan that leaves me.

I linger in the shower, soaking up the hot water. The pressure in my old place was decent, but the water was never hot enough for me. This? It's heaven, and I can see myself getting way too used to it too fast. I lather my sponge up and close my eyes, rubbing it over my body. It feels incredible as I drag it across my breasts and down my stomach, rough but not too rough. If I concentrate really hard, it feels like someone else's hand.

Rhodes' face pops into my head and my eyes fly open.

No. Nope. Not happening.

I barely even finish rinsing before shutting the water off because I am *not* going there. If I'm going to survive living with him, I can't let that happen.

I wrap the softest towel I've ever felt around me and step out of the shower. I take my time rubbing lotion all over my body, then do my nightly skincare routine, trying to let my mind relax so I'm not going to bed thinking about how Rhodes is going to be sleeping just down the hall from me.

Feeling like a brand-new woman, I step out of the bathroom and head into my room.

Poe is skulking around it, and I do my best not to let her out as I slip inside to drop my stuff off. She and Frodo haven't been introduced yet, so I'm trying to keep her in here for now just in case it doesn't go over well.

I dump my dirty clothes into a hamper, then grab my laptop. I'm tired, but just in case I can't sleep in a new house, I'll have my computer so I can edit the makeup tutorial I filmed before heading to Vegas.

Ugh. I don't even want to think about how explosive the comments are going to be after this. I mean, on one hand, it's great for algorithms, but on another…I really hate lying to my subscribers.

I pull open the door and look back at Poe.

She meows, and I instantly feel bad for leaving her in here. She did such a good job on the car ride over and has been stuck in this room all evening.

I'm sure Rhodes won't mind if she sleeps with me, right?

Unable to stop myself, I scoop her up. Just as I'm about to step out of the room, I see my wedding ring lying next to a pile of my things.

Trying not to think too much about it, I slip it on and out the door, then down the hall to Rhodes' bedroom. There's a lump on the couch. All the lights are off, so I assume he's already gone to sleep. I mutter a quick "Good night" as I pass by.

In typical Rhodes fashion, he doesn't respond.

I walk into his bedroom and look around. The room is massive, bigger than my own. The first thing you notice when you walk in is the wall of windows that look out down the hill. There's a perfect line where the sky meets land, and it's gorgeous, almost like a painting.

To one side of the room, there's a bed that's easily four of my old beds put together. To the other, there's a fireplace with two cozy-looking chairs facing it.

And tucked away in the corner is a door that sits ajar, a soft light pouring out of it.

That must be the bathroom.

I note that Rhodes has put a fresh pillow and case at

the end of the bed, and based on the pile of blankets on the chair, it looks like he's put on clean sheets too.

I'm grateful. The last thing I need is to be smelling him all night long.

Poe hops out of my arms to explore, and I set the laptop on the bed, then go to flip the bathroom light off.

Only when I'm just a few feet away do I hear the faint sound of running water.

Oh shit.

Rhodes is in there.

I'm about to retreat and give him his privacy when I catch a glimpse of his very naked backside.

I should pull the door shut and walk away. Cover my eyes. Announce my presence. Literally anything other than standing here and admiring him.

But that's exactly what I do.

He's facing the wall, his head tipped forward as the water cascades over him.

I thought his body was incredible the first time I saw him naked, but seeing him like this is…it's breathtaking.

Like *actually* breathtaking because the air whooshes right from my lungs.

His back is nothing but muscles, and I get now why they call him The Beast.

He's jacked. Completely and totally jacked. I have no clue how he flies down the ice like he does with all those muscles, but it makes it ten times more impressive.

He pushes off the wall, reaching for a bottle of body

wash and his loofa. He suds himself up from head to toe and then…

Holy fuck.

There is no mistaking what he's doing right now.

He palms his cock, and he hisses loudly enough that I hear it over the sound of the water crashing against the floor.

Then he begins to jack himself. Slowly. Very, very slowly.

So slowly there is no way it's not killing him right now.

An ache forms between my legs and I rub them together, trying to ease it. But no matter how much I rub, it doesn't work.

I need more.

Without thinking too much about it, I slip my hand into my sleep shorts and into my underwear. When my finger grazes over my clit, I realize I'm wet just from watching him touch himself.

I had no idea voyeurism was something I was into, but there is no doubt in my mind I could watch this all day long.

I match his long, slow strokes with short, slow circles over my sensitive nub.

When he picks up his pace, I do too.

I sink my teeth into my bottom lip, trying to hold back the noises that are trying to crawl their way from my throat, and when that doesn't work, I slap my hand over my mouth and let them go.

Then, the worst thing possible happens: Rhodes turns around.

I freeze, halting all ministrations.

But he doesn't see me. His eyes are squeezed tightly shut as he leans back against the wall just out from under the water.

No. This is so wrong. I can't do this. I can't stand here watching him bring himself to orgasm while I do the same…right?

But when he begins to jack himself harder, faster, I do the same, rubbing at my clit like I'm about to burst.

He bites down on his lip, his movements growing hastier by the second, and I know he's close. He reaches down with his other hand and gently tugs on his balls.

There is absolutely no mistaking what I hear next.

"*Ryan.*"

It's as clear as if he were standing next to me…and I come apart.

I watch as ropes of cum coat his stomach and his strokes become softer and shorter as his breaths come in sharp succession.

The pounding in my own ears begins to subside as he leans back against the tiled wall, looking spent.

Eyes still closed, he steps back under the water, and I slip away before I'm caught.

I rush out of the room and down the hall to clean off my hand and then tiptoe back into his bedroom and slip beneath the covers, setting my laptop on my lap just as he's pulling open the bathroom door in nothing but a towel.

I avert my eyes to the screen in front of me.

He doesn't seem surprised to see me, and that makes my heart pound all over again.

He scrubs one towel over his head, then walks into the closet without a word. He comes back out wearing a pair of black sweats, tosses his wet towels into the bathroom, and flips the light off.

It's on the tip of my tongue to yell at him for leaving his towel strewn about, but it's not my place.

"Got everything you need?" he asks.

I don't look up from the screen. I can't. I can feel how hot my cheeks are, and there's no way he won't notice the post-orgasm flush I have going on.

"Mhmm," I say as Poe jumps up into the bed beside me, curling into my side.

"All right, then. I'll be out on the couch."

"'Kay."

He hesitates a moment, but when I don't acknowledge, he gives up and heads for the door.

Just as I think he's about to leave without saying anything, he turns back to me and says, "Try not to stay up too late petting your pussy. I'm sure she's tired. It's been quite the day for her. Good night, wife."

And I just know he's not referring to Poe.

CHAPTER 12

RYAN & RHODES

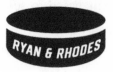

Rhodes: I ordered Chinese.

Ryan: Good for you.

Rhodes: It's here.

Ryan: Cool.

Rhodes: There's enough for two.

Ryan: No, thank you.

Rhodes: Sorry. I don't think I was clear.

. . .

Rhodes: Dinner is here, and you need to come eat.

Ryan: I'm not hungry.

Rhodes: Well, that's too damn bad.

Rhodes: Come eat.

Ryan: No.

Rhodes: Ryan…

Ryan: I'm so glad you know my name.

Rhodes: This is childish. Come eat.

Ryan: No.

. . .

Rhodes: Yes.

Rhodes: I can literally hear your stomach growling right now.

Ryan: Are you standing outside my door?

Rhodes: Yes. Now turn the porn off and come eat.

Ryan: It's not porn.

Rhodes: I am 95% sure I heard moaning.

Rhodes: Unless that was you, then it's totally porn.

Ryan: It's not porn, you ass!

Rhodes: So it's you?

Ryan: OMG NO!

. . .

Ryan: If I agree to come eat, will you leave me alone?

Rhodes: Yes.

Ryan: Fine. I'll be out in a minute.

Rhodes: So you can finish?

Ryan: I seriously hate you.

Rhodes: You only wish you did.

Rhodes: Your sex toy is here.

Ryan: Sex toy?!?

Rhodes: Yeah. Looks like some sort of butt stuff thing.

. . .

Ryan: HAHA

Ryan: Very funny, but that's not my thing.

Rhodes: Duly noted.

Ryan: Besides, whatever it is, it's not mine. I haven't ordered anything since I moved in here.

Rhodes: But you do order sex toys? You just haven't while you've lived here?

Ryan: Of course I order sex toys!

Ryan: But I didn't and that's not mine.

Rhodes: I am looking right at it and it is 100% a sex toy.

Rhodes: I'll send you a pic.

. . .

Ryan: I AM IN THE MIDDLE OF A STORE. DO NOT SEND ME A PICTURE OF A SEX TOY.

Rhodes: *picture*

Rhodes: See? Definitely for your butt or something. There are a ton of attachments.

Ryan: RHODES!

Ryan: That is NOT a sex toy. It's a curling wang, you moron.

Ryan: WAND. Curling WAND.

Rhodes: Sure. Right. Definitely not a "wang" or anything.

Ryan: Just leave it where it is, and I'll grab it when I get home.

. . .

Ryan: Now, can I please finish my shopping in peace?

Rhodes: Yes.

Rhodes: But don't forget to add lube to your list. Looks like you're going to need it.

Ryan: DAMMIT RHODES!

Ryan: Fun fact: Closing the fridge generally helps it stay cold.

Rhodes: Very interesting. I had no idea.

Ryan: Oh, I know you didn't.

Ryan: In case you're not understanding my sarcasm, you left the fridge open when you left this morning. Everything is warm.

. . .

Rhodes: Shouldn't it beep to alert you it's open?? Couldn't you have closed it??

Ryan: Couldn't YOU have closed it?? My milk is all warm and gross.

Rhodes: That's what you get for drinking milk all willy-nilly like some weirdo.

Ryan: It's not willy-nilly. I only drink it when I have pizza or have a lot of chocolate.

Ryan: And don't say willy-nilly. It's weird.

Rhodes: Speaking of a lot of chocolate… Your period chocolates are overflowing the snack cabinet.

Ryan: Those aren't period chocolates. Those are just what I use to cope with the fact that I'm married to you.

Rhodes: Ouch.

. . .

Ryan: Are you going to be home soon?

Rhodes: Missing me already?

Ryan: Not even close.

Rhodes: So planning my murder?

Ryan: Guess you'll never know.

Ryan: I was asking because I was going to make dinner.

Rhodes: You can cook?

Ryan: Never mind.

Rhodes: I'm kidding! What are you making?

Ryan: Parmesan chicken and garlic bread.

. . .

Rhodes: Okay, wow. No need to start talking dirty.

Ryan: I take it that sounds good?

Rhodes: Yes, please.

Ryan: Now who's talking dirty?

Rhodes: Well played.

Rhodes: *picture*

Ryan: I didn't realize we were in the stage of our relationship where we're sending sexy pictures to each other.

Rhodes: Did you just call me sexy?

Ryan: I meant the fact that you're actually following directions and closing the fridge.

. . .

Rhodes: Nope. Sorry. I definitely heard that you think I'm sexy.

Ryan: I definitely didn't say that.

Rhodes: Sure. Whatever you need to tell yourself.

Rhodes: I'm heading to the rink, but I'll be home before lunch. You know, in case you need to take care of yourself because you just can't resist my sexiness.

Ryan: It's not too soon for a divorce, right?

Rhodes: Sorry. You're stuck with me for a whole year. Deal's a deal.

Ryan: Ugh. Don't remind me.

CHAPTER 13

RHODES

She watched.

No—she more than watched.

She *participated.*

I don't know what alerted me to Ryan standing in the bathroom door, but I could just feel her presence. It was like I had conjured her up.

My cock stirred to life when I felt her eyes raking over my body, and I couldn't stop myself from reaching for my dick. I was already aching from the moment we shared in her apartment. There was no way I could stand there and not do anything.

When I heard the soft moans slip through the doorway, I knew she was touching herself too. It took everything I had to keep my eyes closed and not look at her.

I know she heard me say her name. I *wanted* her to hear me say her name. And man, was it worth it.

It's been two weeks and we haven't had a repeat yet. Probably because we went furniture shopping the next day and Ryan has practically been holed up in her room since.

"Please tell me that look on your face isn't what I think it is and you're not thinking naughty thoughts when we're about to help a bunch of kids learn to play hockey."

I glance over at Lowell as he takes a seat beside me on the bench.

"Want me to lie?"

"I swear, you dudes in relationships make me sick."

"I'm not in a relationship."

He slaps his leg. "Oh, right. I forgot. You're fake married. My bad."

"Shut the fuck up, you dick." I glance around, making sure Coach didn't hear anything he said. "Coach doesn't know it's fake."

"I figured as much. How'd he take the news anyway?"

"He's Coach, so about as well as you'd expect."

Coach Heller—or Coach Hell as we call him—is a force to be reckoned with. He might be getting up there in age now, but there's no doubt in my mind that the old enforcer wouldn't strap on a pair of skates and whoop all our asses any day of the week.

"He say anything about Colter?"

"Just don't retaliate."

"The captain in me says that's good advice. But the friend in me…well, it makes me want to wipe the fucking ice with his ass when we play Florida."

I laugh. “Thanks, man.”

“How are things going with the lovely missus anyway?”

Something in the way he says it makes me wonder if he ever had a thing for Ryan. I always thought he might have a crush on her but was too shy to pull the trigger.

That same feeling I had when I saw Miller sitting next to Ryan on the plane streaks through me at the thought of Lowell and Ryan together.

I don’t like the idea one fucking bit.

I push it all aside, not wanting to deal with what it means right now, and shrug. “It’s okay, I guess. We’re mostly still tiptoeing around each other.”

He shakes his head. “I still can’t believe you got drunk married. *You.* I mean, I expect that shit from Miller, but not you.” I glare at him, not appreciating the comparison. “How long are you keeping up the act?”

“A year.”

“A year?” His brows shoot up, and he whistles. “That’s a long time. Think you’ll last that long?”

I do, and that’s solely based on how relieved she was when I told her I’d pay for her grandmother’s care.

Growing up, my parents sacrificed so much for my hockey career, and as much as they tried to hide it, I know what kind of financial burden it was on them. I can’t imagine how Ryan’s felt the last few years taking care of her grandmother. If I can help alleviate that in any way, I’m going to.

My phone buzzes against the bench, pulling my attention.

I look over at the screen. It's a number I don't recognize.

"You going to answer that?"

I shake my head. "Nah. I'll let voicemail get it. Probably nothing important anyway."

I've been getting a lot of calls lately. Most are from people wanting an interview or quote about my recent nuptials. I've ignored them all.

"Rhodes, Lowell, you going to sit around on your asses all day gossiping, or are we going to teach these kids some hockey?" Collin calls from across the ice, throwing his hands in the air and waving 'em like he just don't care.

"You going to let him talk to you like that, captain?" I say to Lowell as we rise onto our skates.

"Not a chance."

Lowell charges toward Collin, who sees him coming, and the two tumble down to the ice, wrestling and trading light punches as the kids cheer them on.

I sigh at their antics and skate past them.

Only in hockey.

The house is quiet when I get home from my evening workout, and I'm not surprised by it one bit. Over the last few weeks, every time I come home, Ryan hides in her bedroom. I'm usually able to coax her out for dinner in the evenings, but it's always like a scene from a movie where the parents who clearly need to be divorced sit at opposite ends of the table and eat in awkward silence.

I think she's still embarrassed by what happened between us that first night.

But something about tonight seems different. Seems off.

I stop at the fridge for a bottle of water, leaning against the counter as I drink it. I listen closely for any signs of movement in the house, but I hear nothing.

Huh. Weird.

After I finish my drink, I toss the bottle into the recycling and head down the hall toward Ryan's room. There's a soft glow of light coming from beneath her door, which isn't atypical.

I rap my knuckles against the wood, but there's no answer.

I knock again. Same response.

"Ryan?" I call out.

Silence.

I push the door open gently, and the moment there's a small crack, Poe darts out of the room, taking off down the hall.

I don't bother chasing after her. She'll find her way back here, I'm sure.

A laptop sitting on the desk in the corner catches my attention.

I shouldn't look at it. I know that.

But I can't stop my feet when they carry me across the room. And I can't help it that my fingers accidentally run across the trackpad, waking the computer up.

The screen comes to life, and a photo fills the screen.

No, not a photo. More than that, it's an invitation to an exhibit featuring photographer Ryan Bell, and it's tonight.

What the…

She has an exhibit? And tonight?

Annoyance races through me, and a little bit of hurt too.

Why the hell wouldn't she tell me about it? I'm her husband, for fuck's sake!

Okay, not *really* her husband, but at the very least, I thought we were friends. I should be there.

I check the time. It's 8:00 PM.

Shit. By the time I get there, it'll be nearly over.

But if I make my shower quick, I should be able to make some of it…

So that's what I do. I rush to my bathroom and hop in the shower, speeding up my routine. When I get out, I dress in one of the suits I wear to my games. I have no idea if this is a black-tie affair, but the word exhibit sounds fancy enough to me and that's what I'm going with.

If she wanted me to show up in anything else, maybe she should have told me about this.

I make sure Poe and Frodo both have food in their bowls, then rush out the door. I hop in my SUV, plug the address into my navigation system, and hit the road.

On the drive there, I run a million reasons through my head for why Ryan wouldn't invite me.

Does she not want to share this part of her with me?

Does she not want me there?

Is she...*embarrassed* by me?

But fuck all of those excuses. I'm going.

I'm going and I will be the best goddamn supportive fake husband there is.

I pull into a parking garage downtown and pay the premium for VIP parking, then walk the block to the studio.

I've walked by this place several times but have never really paid it much attention before. I'm not an artsy type of guy, so it's never been on my radar.

I stop just outside the window to take a peek at the crowd.

Holy shit. The place is packed, and I'm not as mad anymore as pride fills my chest knowing all these people are here for Ryan.

I open the door and soft smooth jazz hits my ears. People turn to stare, and I see the recognition spark in their eyes almost instantly.

Shit. I did not think this part through.

It's a crowd. I fucking hate crowds.

It's funny. Before I got my scar, I had no qualms about being the center of attention. I mean, I was sixteen and a hockey player. I lived for attention.

The moment I walked away from that skate blade, everything changed.

I was still a great hockey player. But more than that, I was a great hockey player with a tragic story, and suddenly everybody cared more about my story than they did my stats.

That was a bitter pill to swallow because I had been playing hockey longer than I'd had my scar. People should have cared about that, not what happened to me. I wanted to quit so many times. Wanted to give up the game I love because I couldn't stand the attention any longer.

But I didn't. And while I still hate the attention, I play anyway.

I might have had my good looks taken away from me, but I'm not going to let this fucking scar steal my love of the game too.

People still hide behind their hands and whisper. They still bring it up all the time. Very few have actually outright asked me about it.

But the thing that hurts the most is the stares.

And that's exactly what I'm getting now.

I don the scowl I'm notorious for and push through the crowd in search of Ryan. Over in the corner, there is a group of people gathered, and I just know in my gut Ryan is at the center of it.

I grab a glass of champagne from one of the waiters strolling around the room and take a healthy drink of it.

Ugh. I fucking hate champagne.

I stand at the periphery of the crowd, watching her command it.

Her blonde hair is twisted into a low-slung bun. It looks messy and elegant all at the same time, and the sudden urge to walk over there, pull it down, and run my fingers through it hits me.

She's wearing a skintight wine-colored satin dress that hits just above her knee. The shade of lipstick painted across her lips matches it perfectly. That same pair of stiletto heels she threw around the hotel room is on her feet, making her legs look a mile long. A dainty pair of diamond earrings hang from her ears, long enough to brush her shoulders, and there's a silver bracelet around her wrist.

Somehow her outfit looks simple and stunning all at once.

She's talking with some older gentleman who keeps putting his hand on her forearm and stepping closer to her despite her continually stepping back. She's smiling politely, but even from here, I can see she's uncomfortable with his closeness.

A protective streak I didn't even know I possessed rushes through me, and before I know it, I'm crossing the small floor and sliding my arm around her waist, hugging her to me.

I instantly feel her relax with my touch. She hasn't even glanced in my direction, yet somehow, she knows it's me.

I like that she knows it's me.

I press a gentle kiss on her cheek. "Hey, wife."

I've called her wife many times, and every time she's looked at me like she wants to strangle me.

Except for now.

The only thing I see in her eyes now is relief. She's glad I'm here.

She grins up at me. "Hey, husband. I'm so glad you could finally make it."

"Sorry. I got held up at the rink." It's not entirely a lie. I was down at the practice facility in the weight room and time did get away from me. I squeeze her waist. "But I'm here now. You look stunning."

Her eyes spark with surprise at my compliment because she can tell it's genuine.

"Thank you," she says, and I see the blush steal up her cheeks.

I turn to the older gentleman who kept touching her, sticking my hand out and rising to my full height. I tower over him with ease. "I don't think we've had the pleasure of meeting yet. I'm Adrian Rhodes, Ryan's husband."

He must know who I am because his eyes flare with interest as he slips his hand in mine. "Wow. The Beast in the flesh. My son is going to be so jealous I'm meeting you." He looks between Ryan and me. "I had no idea you two were married."

"Newly married," Ryan explains.

"And wildly in love." I place a loud, wet kiss to her cheek. "Right, baby cakes?"

Ryan's lips tighten at the nickname, but only for a

second. Then, she beams at me and places her hand on my chest, snuggling closer to me. "So in love, honey bun."

"How…sweet." He gives us a curt smile, then excuses himself.

The moment he's out of earshot, Ryan puts a bit of space between us. "Baby cakes? Wildly in love? Really?"

"Just staking my claim."

"Claim, huh?"

"Yes." I drop my lips to her ear and hear the hitch in her breath when my lips graze across her skin. "This marriage might not be traditional, but make no mistake—you're mine for the next year."

She lets out a little squeak, and I can see the goose bumps break out across her body. She recovers quickly, bringing the champagne flute to her lips, but with the way the liquid shakes in her glass, it's obvious she's rattled.

I straighten back up and look out over the crowd. "Thanks for the invite, by the way."

"I…I didn't think you'd want to come."

I pinch my eyebrows together. "Why wouldn't I want to come? You're my wife."

"You hate crowds."

"I'd sit in a crowd of a hundred thousand people if it meant being there to support you."

She seems surprised by this, and honestly, I'm surprised too because I actually mean the words.

Her photography is important to her, so it's

important to me. Besides, she's putting herself out there in a very public way to support my hockey career. This is the least I can do for her.

"Well, thank you," she says quietly. "I appreciate that."

"You're welcome. And next time, invite me."

"Okay."

For the first time, a comfortable silence falls over us.

I take another sip of my champagne and make a face. *Fuck, I really hate this stuff.*

"So, this…show," I say. "What exactly is it?"

"It's an interactive exhibit."

"Like the one you did with Harper and Collin?"

"Sort of. This one is about something different though."

"What's that?"

"It's…" She hesitates for a moment. "It's about flaws." I stiffen at her words. "And finding the beauty in them." Her eyes flit toward my scar. "Because they're all beautiful."

"Is that so?"

She nods. "Yes. And I prove it to the subjects by putting their images up for sale. With their permission, of course. And they do. Sell, I mean."

"Hmm."

"Would you like to try it?"

I don't answer her because I'm stunned by her request.

"You don't have to, of course. It's just…well, I would

just like to photograph you. If you'd let me." She tucks an errant strand of hair behind her ear, not making eye contact with me. She's nervous. Ryan doesn't do nervous.

I'm speechless. She wants to photograph…me?

"I'm sorry," she says. "Forget I asked. I'm going to…" Her words trail off as she begins to walk away.

I don't let her.

I wrap my hand around her wrist and tug her back to me.

She peers up, her green eyes round with surprise.

"Yes."

"Pardon?"

"Yes." I swallow the sudden lump in my throat. "You can photograph me."

I don't know why I say it. I think it's the sincerity in her eyes. Either way, it's out there now, and I can't take it back. Not when she's looking at me with pure excitement at the idea.

"Follow me."

I let her lead me to the other side of the room. We're stopped a few times by people who want to congratulate her on her exhibit that's wrapping up. When we finally make it over there, she tugs me inside the little makeshift room.

The moment we step inside, it's complete silence.

"Soundproof," she explains, locking the door behind her. "So there are no distractions."

I nod. "Makes sense."

The space is much longer and narrower than I

expected it to be. And the only thing inside is this single stall toward the back and Ryan's camera.

"The idea of the project is that I ask people what they believe their flaws are, and I photograph them."

"So, what? You just take pictures of people's imperfections?"

"Yes, but we have to remember that not everyone's flaws are external. Some people have internal flaws. The subject takes a seat at the stool across the room. I'll ask a few questions to start, and then from there, you can either show me your flaws or you can talk about them. Either way, I'll be capturing the whole experience on video and taking photos."

I nod. "I see. And the purpose of this is…?"

"Sometimes we just need to see ourselves from a different angle. Through someone else's eyes."

"That seems simple enough."

I cross the small room, stopping right in front of the stool.

My hands are shaking just the slightest bit, and I shove them in my pockets so she doesn't see.

I'm nervous, which is ridiculous really because it's pretty damn obvious what my biggest flaw is.

She watches me closely, finger poised and ready to press record.

I can tell she's conflicted inside. The photographer in her is thrilled to have another subject, but the people part of her knows this is hard on so many levels.

Finally, I take a seat.

"Things might get a little awkward at home afterward."

Her brows draw tight together. "Why is that?"

"Well, because I have to whip my dick out."

She sputters. "W-What?"

I nod solemnly. "Yeah. My cock. It's just...*huge*. So heavy to carry around. A burden, really. Definitely my biggest flaw."

"See, I would have thought it was your not-so-sparkling personality."

"Not-so-sparkling? You're telling me you don't see the rainbows and glitter always shooting out my ass?"

She tucks her lips together, crossing her arms over her chest. "Are you quite finished, Rhodes?"

"Yes, ma'am." I wink at her, the tension in the room now thinned. I rub my hands over my thighs and nod once. "Hit record."

There's a barely audible click as she presses the button and a red light sparks to life. They're the only indications that she's recording.

"What is your name, age, and occupation?"

"My name is Adrian Tyler Rhodes. I am twenty-seven years old, and I am an NHL defenseman for the Carolina Comets."

"Do you believe you are flawed, Adrian?"

I don't know why, but hearing her say my first name does something to me that I'm not expecting. In the time I've known her, not once has she called me Adrian. And to my surprise, I like it.

I don't look at the camera; I look at her. "Aren't we all flawed in one way or another?"

"I suppose so. Is that why you're here though? Because you're flawed?"

"Honestly, I'm just here so I can get my wife to show me her titties later tonight."

"Even the wonky one?"

"*Especially* the wonky one."

She barely holds in her laughter. "If this goes well, I'm sure she'll take that into consideration."

"So behave? Got it."

She shakes her head, smiling. "If you had to pick out a singular flaw for yourself, what would it be?"

I clear my throat and look away from her penetrating gaze. I tug at my dress pants, that nervous itchy feeling returning. "I think it's pretty obvious, no?"

"Not to me."

My gaze snaps back to hers, and somehow, I know it's not photographer Ryan talking to me; it's the Ryan I know.

"It happened during a routine practice the summer I turned sixteen. It was at a sleepaway hockey camp I attended every year. I knew that place like the back of my hand, and I knew the players out there with me. They were all good guys. Nobody would ever intentionally hurt anyone else, and that day was no different. We were running board drills and I guess I lost an edge, and I went down. Unfortunately for me, the guy I was running the drill with didn't realize I went down. His focus was solely on getting the puck out, just like it should have been. His skate came back and it caught me right under the visor, sliced me from here"—I point to the spot just below my eye—"to here." I drag my finger along the scar, stopping where it ends at my chin.

I hear the click of the camera as I move my fingers and try hard not to flinch.

"What happened after that?" Ryan asks, still clicking away.

"I…I don't remember." I run a hand through my hair. "I think I passed out pretty quick. Shock, blood loss…I have no clue. I woke up in the hospital looking like a monster." I huff out a humorless laugh. "My face was a disaster, puffy and bruised. I looked just like you'd imagine. God, I remember the look on my mom's face when I woke up. She was so fucking relieved that I was alive. And I was relieved too, ya know? I was okay. I still had my vision. I would still play hockey. But then when I looked in the mirror, I…"

I clear my throat, trying hard as hell to ignore the way it's tightening.

"The hockey camp was out in the middle of nowhere, and the doctor at the nearest hospital completely botched fixing it. He'd never seen anything like it before and had no clue what he was doing. I had two plastic surgeries to fix it, and I still fucking look like this."

All those same feelings from back then come rushing in.

"Before that, I wasn't one to obsess about my looks. I was an average-looking kid who blended in with the crowd. But after…after I was this whole new person. Suddenly, I wasn't average. I was disfigured and ugly. Little kids in the stores would stare at me, and my friends stopped wanting to be seen with me. My scar was all I was. And sometimes…" I exhale shakily. "Sometimes I think it's all I'll ever be. I'm going to carry this…ugliness around with me forever. Who the fuck wants to love a beast like me?"

Ryan sets her camera aside, then crosses the small room.

She doesn't stop until she's standing between my legs. She takes my face in her hands, running her thumb gently over my scar and the tears that are dripping down my cheeks.

I didn't even realize I was crying. Why the fuck am I crying?

She leans forward and presses her lips to the jagged, marred skin.

She's kissing it. She's fucking kissing my scar.

She's kissing my scar, and she's kissing my soul.

"Adrian…" She whispers my name, trailing her lips across the part of me I hate the most and somehow making me hate it less. "You're beautiful. Not despite your scar, but because of it."

They're the same words she said to me that night in Vegas. I wasn't sure she meant them then, but I know she means them now.

I swallow thickly. "Ryan?"

"Yes?"

"That kissing rule...you said I could only kiss you if it's warranted, right?"

"Yes."

"Does this count as warranted?"

She sighs against me. "Yes."

And I claim my kiss.

CHAPTER 14

RYAN

Everything else ceases to exist.

The only thing that matters at this moment is Rhodes and the way his mouth is moving against mine.

I know he joked before about his kisses being good and like sex, but I'm starting to think he wasn't too far off the mark.

If this is how it feels just to *kiss* Rhodes, I can't wait for more.

My fingers brush along his face, wiping away the tears I don't think he realized he was shedding. His story…it almost broke me. He was so raw and real and open. It was a side of him I've never seen before.

And it was a side of him I'd like to see again.

His fingers dig into my hips as he tugs me closer. Slowly, he bunches up the material, dragging it up my waist until I feel the cool air on my bare ass. All the while his mouth is moving over mine in perfect strokes.

His hands run over my bare ass, and I moan.

He breaks the kiss for the first time, peering up at me with glassy eyes.

"Are you wearing underwear, Ryan?"

I shake my head. "No. Didn't want panty lines."

A low growl rumbles through his chest. "You left the house without panties?" I nod, and he glowers at me. "I don't like that."

"I don't care what you like," I say, lifting a challenging brow.

His eyes darken as he lifts my dress higher until my pussy is exposed, not stopping until it's bunched around my waist. I shiver as the cool air hits me.

His hands knead at my cheeks, then he rubs down my thighs, digging his fingers into me just enough that it stings a little.

"God, you smell so fucking good." He nuzzles his nose against my stomach, inhaling me. He nips at me a bit, licking away the stings with short strokes as I slide my hands through his hair.

"No one can see us in here, right?"

"No. Nor hear us."

"Good." He places a kiss just below my belly button, then slides off the stool and onto his knees right in front of me. "Spread your legs, darling. I need to taste you."

For once, I don't hate the pet name…and I do as I'm told.

I widen my stance and close my eyes, waiting.

But nothing happens.

I look down and he's just sitting there, staring up at me.

"That's much better."

I furrow my brow. "Huh?"

"If you want me to eat your pussy, you'll have to watch. Got it?"

Oh. *Oh.*

I gulp, nodding. "Okay."

"No. Say *Yes, husband.*"

Another gulp. "Yes, husband."

"Very good."

Without breaking eye contact, he flattens his tongue and runs it over my clit. My eyes begin to flutter closed at just the barest of touches, and he backs off.

I want to scream in frustration, but I also want to please him.

I open my eyes again, and he grins wickedly, then returns between my legs.

This time, I make sure to follow directions. I don't close my eyes. I don't even dare blink.

I hold his gaze as he laps at me. Stroke after torturous stroke, his hands kneading my ass cheeks over and over again until I'm literally bucking against him.

Even though I'm looking right at him, I don't see it coming.

I let out a loud yelp that turns into a moan as he lands a loud *thwack* to my bare ass.

My eyes flare as he grins up at me around my pussy as he massages my no-doubt-red stinging cheek.

He remembers.

Rhodes lands another blow, then another, and my knees begin to shake so violently I have no idea how I'm still standing.

How? How is it possible he has me this close to the edge so quickly? It's like he's inside my head and knows just exactly what I like. There's no way anything can compare to this.

He smacks my ass again, and I know I'm seconds away from an orgasm.

He knows it too.

He sucks my clit into his mouth, applying the perfect amount of pressure, then smacks my ass again.

I break.

I'm rocked by the most intense orgasm of my life, my legs quaking so hard I can barely stand. Rhodes has to physically hold me up.

I ride the wave as he continues to gently lick at me. With one last long, slow stroke, he sits back on his haunches.

His eyes are darker than I've ever seen before, and his face is shining with the evidence of my orgasm. I'm incredibly turned on by the sight and am slightly sad when he wipes the back of his hand across it.

He rises to his feet, keeping his hands on my waist because even he knows if he lets me go, there's no way I'll be able to stay upright.

He presses gentle kisses up across my jaw and down my neck, then back up until he captures my lips. He gives me a quick peck, then pulls back, cradling my face and tilting it up.

"Thank you," he says quietly.

Thank me? Pfft. I should be thanking him.

"Thank you for letting me tell you my story."

Oh. That.

I wrap my arms around his waist, holding him close. "Thank you for telling me. And for the orgasm."

He chuckles. "Trust me, the pleasure was all mine. But, Ryan?"

"Yeah?"

"I still definitely want to see your titties when we get home."

Sitting through the rest of my exhibit was torture. Cleaning up afterward? Even worse.

And it's all because of the looks Rhodes kept sending my way.

Every time I looked at him, I blushed. Having his eyes on me was a permanent reminder of what we did in the booth. And a reminder of how badly I wanted to do it again.

When we finally push through the front door of the house, I am more than ready to rip my clothes off and let him have his way with me.

Apparently, he has the same idea.

The door isn't even latched, and he has me pinned

against the wall, my dress hiked back up around my hips and one of my legs thrown around his waist. Based on the way his cock is pressing against my core, he wants this just as badly as I do.

His lips find my neck and he bites and sucks at me. I just know I'm going to have marks tomorrow. At this point, I don't care.

He claims my mouth again, his hand climbing up my throat, applying just enough pressure to make my knees shake with desire.

"Please," I beg. "I need…"

"What? What do you need?" he says against me. "Tell me what you need."

"You. Just you."

He crashes his mouth to mine and palms my ass, pulling me up until I wrap my legs around his waist. He carries us down the hall, not stopping until we reach his bedroom. With my legs still around him, he puts one knee on the foot of his bed, slowly dropping me onto my back.

He wrenches his mouth from mine.

"I want to savor you and devour you all at once."

I want that too. But I say, "Devour now. Savor later."

So he does.

He shoves his suit jacket off, then undoes his pants, pushing them down just enough to free that damn beautiful cock of his.

I want to see it. I want to *taste* it.

But not now.

Now, I just want him.

He bunches my dress around my waist and then slips his hand between my legs.

"So wet," he mutters. "So fucking wet and so fucking perfect."

He wraps one arm around me, his hand fisting my hair. With the other, he lines his cock up with my core, then pushes inside me.

There's no preamble. No going slow.

We are straight-up fucking at this point, and it's just what I need.

I slide my hands into his hair, tugging at the strands and pulling his lips down to mine as he slams into me over and over again.

I need to kiss him. Need to feel him fuck my mouth with his tongue as he fucks my pussy with his cock.

"Holy shit," he moans, breaking the kiss but not his stride. "You feel fucking incredible. Better than I imagined."

"You've imagined me?"

He gives me a look. "You know I have." He ruts into me again. "You know I do."

He kisses me again, slowing his movements. But I don't want slow. I want fast. I want hard. I want more.

I try to pick up the pace, but he doesn't let me.

"Stop," he says against my lips. "I'm seriously about to embarrass myself if we keep this up."

"It's fine, Rhodes."

"It's not."

I pull away, grabbing his face, brushing my thumb against his scar. "It's. Fine. I want this. *Please.* Fuck me."

That same rumbly growl from earlier moves through him again, and he strokes in and out of me with a newfound purpose.

I can feel my orgasm building. Getting closer and closer to that sweet, sweet high.

I just need…

Like he can read my mind, Rhodes slips his hand between us, his thumb pressing against my clit as he bucks into me.

Oh. That.

I count down in my head.

One.

Two.

And I explode.

I squeeze my eyes shut as my pussy clenches around him. Rhodes lets out a string of cuss words, and I know he's not far behind at all.

"Oh, fuck. No. Fuck, fuck."

"What?" I ask. Or at least I think it sounds like *what.* My brain is so scrambled right now I can't tell up from down.

"Condom—I forgot a condom."

"Birth control. I have an implant. Recent checkup. All good."

He laughs. "You're talking in caveman, and it's kind of doing things to me."

"Shut up."

"I'm good too. We get tested regularly by the doc."

I nod because it's all I can muster at this point.

"You know," he says, "at least if you did get pregnant, it wouldn't be out of wedlock."

I groan. "Rhodes…"

"What? I'm just saying."

"I swear…I'll—*Oh!* Holy fuckinggoddamn-shitballsfuck!"

"That's a mouthful. Rhodes will do just fine." His thumb is back on my clit and he's hitting that *just right* angle inside of me.

"Don't stop. What you're doing right now, do. Not. Stop."

He doesn't.

And before I know it, I'm going off again, and this time he follows right along behind me.

Just like there was no real beginning, there's no real end.

Rhodes rolls off me, and all that can be heard is our harsh breaths echoing around the room.

I'm pretty sure I died.

I must have. There's no way I can have three orgasms in a night and this not be heaven.

"Are we dead?"

The bed shakes with his laughter. "I think so. Oddly enough, I'm okay with it."

"Same."

His hand finds mine and he tangles our fingers together. He rubs at my wedding ring like he always does.

"I hate to bring this up to you right now, but I told you you'd want me."

I roll my eyes. "Shut up, Rhodes."

Somehow—and I don't know how he does it—he rolls over until he's hovering just above me.

He grins down at me. "Make me…*wife*."

And I do.

When I wake with an arm wrapped tightly around my waist, déjà vu washes over me.

I've been here before. This same position with this same person.

Except this time, I don't regret waking up this way.

Rhodes tightens his arm around me and drags me as he rolls over, and suddenly, I'm right back where I started—straddling him topless.

"I swear, if you make one comment about my wonky tit, I'm going to poke you in the eye with it."

He grins, not opening his eyes. "If you think that's a threat, it's really not."

"It should be."

"But it's not." He squeezes my ass, peeling his eyes open slowly. "How the hell are you awake right now? We barely slept last night."

I shrug. "Woke up to something poking me in the back."

"Wonder what that could be." He shoves his hips up, pushing said *something* against me.

"Does that thing even work anymore?"

"Not sure. Want to test it out?"

I groan, then roll off him. "No way. I'm sore in places I didn't even realize I could be sore."

"Huh, really? Because I distinctly remember you saying no to anal."

I side-eye him. "Funny." I push myself up, resting back against the headboard. "I wasn't kidding. Everything hurts right now. My legs, my arms, my pussy. I feel like I did a weightlifting competition or something."

He sits up next to me, hooking his arms behind his head. "It's times like these it pays to be a hockey player. I've got stamina for days."

"Are you always this gloaty after sex?"

"Nah." He gives me a lopsided grin. "Just after really good sex."

I grin. Good answer.

But it is weird to see him so…chipper.

I'm used to grumpy Rhodes, not smiley Rhodes.

"Don't worry. I'll be back to my grumpy self shortly," he promises, like he can read my mind.

Speaking of grumpy Rhodes…

I spring from the bed, new life breathed into me, and take off toward the living room. He calls after me, but I ignore him and head straight for my camera bag.

I didn't get a chance to look over the photos from last

night, and I'm dying to see how they turned out. I flip through the images until I come across the set of Rhodes.

I gasp the moment I see them.

He looks…*heartbreaking.* And haunting. And so fucking beautiful.

"Hey," he says, padding into the living room. "Where'd you go?"

I push up from my crouch and wave my camera at him.

"The photos from last night—I wanted to see them."

A conflicted look flits across his face. I can tell a part of him wants to see them and a part of him doesn't want to be reminded of his scar at all.

But he *needs* to see these. I can sense it in my gut.

I navigate back to the first one and turn my camera toward him. His fingers tremble as he takes it from me, but I don't dare say anything about it. I watch him as he clicks through slowly. He takes his time looking at them all, studying them.

When he gets to the last one, he closes his eyes.

It's the one of him crying.

After several moments, he peels his eyes open, looking down at me. "Is this…is this how you see me?"

I nod. "I meant it when I said you were beautiful, Rhodes. I wish you could see that too."

"But my scar. It's…"

"Part of you but not all of you."

His throat bobs. "I…"

He looks away, running the palm of his hand over his face and sniffling.

"Fuck," he mutters. When he looks back at me, his eyes are shiny with unshed tears. "Thank you, Ryan."

"No, thank *you*. Thank you for showing me the real you. It's about time I got to meet him."

Without another word, he scoops me into his arms and carries me back to the bedroom.

I have no idea how long we stay there, but I know it's not long enough.

CHAPTER 15

RHODES

"Come on, Batesy, let's pick it up!"

"I'm trying, Coach!"

I shake my head at the lip the kid is giving me. "He's skating like shit."

"Dude, he's like ten," Smith, the oldest guy on our team and one of our best centers, reminds me.

"So? I could skate way better than that at ten. I swear, it's the water these kids are drinking nowadays. It's too clean. They just need a good old-fashioned sip out of a water hose."

"Okay, grandpas," Miller says, skating by us.

I glare at him. "You know what? You go skate too. You need the practice."

"And a lesson to not back talk your elders."

"You got *elders* right," he sasses back at Smith. "I could skate laps around both of you."

"Maybe, but would you care to wager on who could throw the heaviest punch?" I ask, taking a step toward him.

I swear I hear his asshole pucker. "You know what? I think a few laps *do* sound good."

Huh. Maybe Miller is smarter than he looks.

"That's what I thought, rookie," I call after him as he skates off down the ice.

Smith chuckles, shaking his head. "Kid exhausts me."

"Same."

"By the way, I've been meaning to tell you congratulations on the whole marriage thing. Sorry I didn't get you a gift, but I guess it was kind of last minute, huh? I will say, I'm surprised you got hitched. Didn't really expect that one."

"Bit of a surprise for me too," I mutter, but can't help the grin that stretches across my lips. It might have been a surprise, but I can't say I'm hating it so far.

Especially not the whole waking up with a naked Ryan in my bed every morning part.

"It looks good on you though. Marriage, I mean. You look happy for a change. Guess that makes me the grumpy one now, huh?"

He wasn't always like that, but last season something in him changed. You think winning the Cup would get him out of his funk, but he can't seem to shake it.

I want to ask him what's up, but I don't want to press. Smith is definitely the type of guy who will let you know when he's ready to talk, and right now, he's not.

He claps me on the shoulder, then nods toward Miller. "I'm gonna go make sure the rookie isn't corrupting the children."

Smith skates away and Collin takes his place.

"How long have you been lurking there?" I ask him.

"Long enough. He was right, you know. Marriage *does* look good on you."

"Shut up," I grumble.

Collin laughs. "How are things going with Ryan anyway?"

Things with Ryan are…incredible.

She's incredible.

I can't remember the last time she spent the night in her own room, or the last time she hid away to only come out for dinner.

And it's not even the out-of-this-world sex that makes everything so incredible. It's like whatever happened between us the night of her exhibit a few weeks ago changed everything.

Things have been good. Easy. Simple.

I like good and easy and simple, especially in a situation as complicated as this.

Neither of us have talked about exactly what it is we're doing, but I'm okay with that because I'm not sure I'm ready to dissect it.

"Oh, I take it they *are* good, then," Collin says.

I glance over at him. "What do you mean? I didn't even say anything."

"Trust me, bud. You didn't have to. It's obvious you're in love."

I glower. "Fuck off. I am not."

"Yes, you are. And that's cool. Totally fine. I mean, a

little backassward that you fell in love with your wife *after* you married her, but still cool."

"I'm not in love with her," I say through clenched teeth.

He pats me on the back. "Right. Sure."

"Stop fucking patronizing me."

He holds his hands up innocently. "I'm not."

"You are."

"No, I'm not."

"You are fucking too."

He smirks. "See how annoying it is when people lie straight to your face?"

I charge at him, not stopping until our noses are nearly touching. He just laughs.

"Be nice. The kids are watching."

"Good. Maybe they can learn a thing or two about chirping a guy who is bigger than them."

"I'm not scared of you, Rhodes."

"You fuckin' ought to be, Wright."

"Guys, come on," Lowell hollers across the ice. "Not in front of the lady."

I spin on my skates to find Ryan standing beside Lowell.

I almost forgot she was coming today to photograph the kids during their last day of camp. We start our NHL version of hockey camp here next week, and I can't wait. That buzz I love from playing the game is beginning to simmer in my veins.

Hockey season is so close I can almost taste it, and damn am I hungry for it.

I skate across the ice, stopping in front of Lowell and Ryan.

She grins at me, looking absolutely adorable in her puffy gray jacket and beanie with the little fuzzy ball on top.

"Wife," I say.

"Husband," she responds, her cheeks growing pink.

"Gag," Lowell comments, hopping onto the ice to go round up the kids, I'm sure.

"How's your day, snookums?" I ask her once we're alone.

"Just wonderful, schmoopy."

"Schmoopy? Really?"

"I could say the same about snookums."

Unable to help myself, I lean across the boards and press my lips to hers in a quick kiss.

She gasps, surprised.

I'm surprised too. I'm not one for PDA even in a real relationship, so I'm surprised I'm doing it in a fake one. I can't seem to control myself when it comes to Ryan though, and I've not determined yet if that's a good or bad problem to have.

My phone buzzes against the bench, pulling my attention, and Ryan points to it.

"That yours?"

"Yeah, but it's probably just a spam call. I've been

getting a lot of them lately." I let it go to voicemail. "Did you get those tutorials edited today?"

She nods. "Yep. Two of them."

It's kind of weird knowing a person who does YouTube for a living. Some days I'll come home, and Ryan won't be wearing a stitch of makeup. Other days she looks like a zombie—literally.

But she seems to enjoy what she does, and that's all that matters. I'll never admit this to anyone, but sometimes when she's asleep, I go on there and watch them just to help her with views.

"And I took Frodo out for a walk. Oh! They did it again! You have to see!" She pulls her phone out and taps around a few times, then shoves it in my face. "Aren't they so cute?!"

We were worried Poe and Frodo wouldn't get along well, so we made sure to introduce them slowly. Turns out, we didn't have to worry about a thing. This is now the third time we've caught them snuggled up together in Frodo's bed. I'm glad he'll have a friend in Ryan and Poe while I'm away for hockey games.

"I'm pretty sure Poe loves Frodo more than me now."

"Well, that's not a big feat. Have you seen Frodo?"

She pushes her chest out. "Okay, but have you seen me and my sweet, sweet rack?"

"A few times." I shrug. "Not bad."

Her brows crash together. "Not bad? *Not bad?!*"

"I've seen worse, I've seen better."

"Adrian…" she warns.

"It kind of turns me on when you call me by my first name."

"What about shithead? Does it turn you on when I call you shithead?"

"You know, can't say it does. No."

"You are so—"

I lean over and kiss her again, slanting my mouth over hers and claiming her for all to see.

She moans into my mouth, and just when I'm about to deepen the kiss, it's ruined.

"All right, all right. Break it up. There are children present."

"Yeah, *Adrian*, there are kids here." Ryan giggles.

"Little cockblockers," I mumble before turning around. "Okay, everyone gather around." I point at Ryan. "This is Ryan, my wife, and she's going to be taking our group photo today, so everyone be on your best behavior or it's me you'll be answering to, got it?"

They all nod, totally afraid of me just like I like them to be.

When I turn around, Ryan's staring at me with a look I don't quite understand.

"What?" I ask.

"Nothing. It's nothing." She shakes her head, then smiles. "All right, everyone, this is how I want you…"

As she directs the kids where she wants them, Lowell and Collin skate up to me, one on each side.

"Your *wife*, huh?" Collin says.

"Yeah. That's what she is."

"Is she though? Because I thought—"

"Watch it," I say, nodding toward Miller.

"Oh, Lowell, you didn't hear?" Collin says. "Our little Rhodes here is totally in love with his *wife*."

I sigh, pinching the bridge of my nose between my thumb and forefinger. "Collin. I swear…"

"I'm still not scared, Rhodes."

"Fuckin' should be," I mutter.

"You two still hosting that party this weekend so we can all come over and meet your *wife*?"

"Quit saying it like that."

"Like what?"

"Like it's…"

"Like it's what?" Lowell leans into me. "Fake?"

I scowl, and they both laugh.

"Oh, yeah, he's totally in love," Lowell agrees.

"Truly."

"Madly."

"Deeply."

"Okay, Savage Garden, that's enough!" I bark. "Fuck. You two almost make me want to hang out with the rookie."

"Who, me?" Miller says, skating up to us. "I'll be your dream, I'll be your wish, I'll be your fantasy!" he sings.

I shove past him, skating away from all three of the assholes.

"What? I thought we were singing!" Miller calls after me. "I still need to be your hope, love, and everything you need!"

I flip them off.

They're all wrong.

"Dude, who brought the old broad? She's a hoot."

Lowell groans. "Jesus, Miller, show some respect. This is Grams, Ryan's grandmother. Grams, this is Miller, our resident rookie."

"Oh shit. I mean SHOOT. SORRY, GRAMS."

"Um, why are you shouting at my grandmother? She can hear perfectly fine."

Grams pats Miller on the cheek. "I am so glad you're good at hockey, son. Don't lose that skill. You're going to need it."

Miller blushes. "Thank you, ma'am?" It comes out as a question because he has no idea if he's just been insulted or not.

Spoiler alert: he has been.

Grams is…well, she's fucking amazing. Basically an older version of Ryan.

We got her moved into a new assisted living facility last week, and I about shit myself when I saw the price. Not because I couldn't afford it. I mean, I have enough money to last me a lifetime. I was shocked that Ryan had been making payments like that for years.

Grams has only been in the new place a week, but she seems like she's thriving there. Ryan said her attitude has improved by leaps and bounds. And really, as long as she's happy, I don't care how much I'm paying for it.

By some miracle, we were able to keep our *Oh hey, we got hitched*-slash-*end of summer* party to a minimum number of guests. Most people wanted to stay home with their families before all the real chaos starts next week.

The party has dwindled to just the main crew now. We are currently sitting outside at the patio table, shooting the shit.

Collin keeps looking over here smirking at me, and I think it's because Ryan is sitting on my lap.

I have no idea why she is. I don't even think *she* knows why she is. But I'm not about to change it.

"So, are you boys ready for the season?" Grams asks.

According to Ryan, she's become a big hockey fan in recent years. I guess that means we're going to have to get her out to a game soon. It would be fun to see her in the stands one night.

"Back-to-back, baby!" Miller shouts, holding his beer up.

He's convinced we're going back-to-back with the Cup championship.

I'm trying not to jinx it, and I think that's how a lot of the other guys on the team feel about it too.

"We're ready, Viv," Collin says. "You're coming to our home opener, right?"

"And see my guys in action? I wouldn't miss it."

"She just wants to see some hockey butts," Harper says, nudging her. "Right, Grams?"

"Well, heck yeah, girl. You know all about them. Your man has a dump truck."

"Grams!" Ryan reprimands. "What the…"

"What? That's what my new roommate, Nancy, says you call a nice, big hockey butt."

"Please tell Nancy I said thank you, and remind me to bring her a signed jersey next time." Collin grins, quite proud of himself.

"Nancy also said Lowell has 'BDE,' but I don't know what that means."

"Can confirm," Lowell says.

"And that she was 'DTF,' which I guess means 'down to flirt,' with Rhodes."

"GRANDMOTHER!" Ryan screeches, her face turning redder than I've ever seen before as we all snicker.

"What?" Grams holds her hands out, perplexed by Ryan's reaction. "I'm just trying to warn you that Nancy is trying to flirt with your man."

"Bet you won't fight her, Ryan," Collin says.

"Shit, my money is on Nancy."

Ryan glares at Lowell. "You're just saying that because she's in love with your you know what." She bends her head toward me, lowering her voice to a whisper. "That's it. We're moving her back to the other place. I can't handle her knowing all these slang words. That place is going to corrupt my sweet grandmother."

"Hate to break it to you, but I'm pretty sure your grandmother has *been* corrupted," I say back quietly.

"The first time we met, she pinched my ass and blamed it on the sleeping lady next to her."

Ryan rolls her lips together, trying not to laugh. "Well, that's your fault for having such a pinchable dump truck."

"Keep it up, wife, and I'll give Nancy a call."

"You wouldn't dare."

"Guess we'll never know." I wink, squeezing her hip and taking a sip of my beer.

I was dreading today, was certain hosting this little party would be exhausting and sitting here pretending to be married to Ryan and lying to all our friends would be hard.

Except it wasn't exhausting. Not at all.

Because the truth is…I'm not so sure we're pretending anymore.

CHAPTER 16

RYAN

Rhodes' parents are going to be here any second, and I could vomit.

It's one thing to pretend to be married in front of our friends—it oddly didn't even feel pretend at all—but it's a whole other thing to pretend in front of his parents.

I think another reason I'm feeling a little sick is that tomorrow Rhodes has his first game of the season, and I'm genuinely nervous for him.

Before Harper met Collin, I wouldn't have been able to tell you a single thing about hockey other than that the players are known for having great butts. But watching Rhodes prep for the season over the last few weeks has been so fascinating. His routines. The way he gets into his head and focused on the game. It's all so…intense. I mean, Rhodes is an intense person in general, but this is different.

There's also a small part of me that's a little sad hockey season is about to officially kick off. I actually missed him when he was gone for preseason games.

I wouldn't dare tell him that though. He'll let it go to his head.

I hear the garage door open, and I freeze in my tracks.

Oh no. They're here.

"I'm not ready!" I yell to a still empty house.

But it doesn't matter if I'm ready or not. It's happening.

"Well, this doesn't look good at all."

I whirl around to find Rhodes standing in the open garage doorway.

He's looking back and forth between the item I'm holding and my wide eyes.

"Are you that nervous that you're drinking this early?"

"What?" I chuckle, then cover my mouth because it *sounds* nervous. *I* sound nervous. Which doesn't make me look suspiciously drunk at all. I tuck the bottle of wine I'm holding behind my back. "I wasn't drinking it, I swear. I was panic cleaning and remembered I left it in the freezer last night and I was moving it to the fridge."

"Panic cleaning?"

"Yeah, you know, that thing you do right before someone comes over."

"Why are you panic cleaning? We have housekeepers."

"Because I'm nervous!"

"Nervous? What's there to be nervous about?" Rhodes' mother elbows past him and into the house, sending him a dirty look. "Oh, for heaven's sake, go help your father unload the car."

She continues into the kitchen, heading straight for me.

Then, she wraps me up in the warmest hug I've ever had and squeezes me tight.

It's heaven. Actual heaven.

"Oh. My. Goodness. It is *so* nice to finally meet you!"

I squeeze her back just as tight. "Me? Pfft. It's so great to finally meet *you*, Margaret!"

She's a petite woman with a soft middle. Her hair is the same tawny color as Rhodes' and hangs in loose curls just beyond her shoulders. Her eyes are a warm brown and her smile is bright enough to warm the room as she beams at me.

"Call me Maggie," she says. "You are family after all."

She hesitates on the word family just the slightest, and I can hardly blame her for that. With how suddenly Rhodes and I got married, it's no wonder she'd have trouble using that term.

"I can't wait to get to know you. Rhodes has told me so much about you." *He has?* She laughs. "Oh, I can see the worry in your eyes." She pats my cheek. "There's nothing to be afraid of. It was all good things."

Now I'm wondering what exactly it is he told her.

"Ha. I hope so. Rhodes speaks very highly of you and Oscar as well."

She blushes when I say her husband's name like she's

still completely smitten with him. It's sweet. I want something like that.

For the briefest moment, I imagine what that could be like with Rhodes. If he would still be smitten with me like that years later.

But I brush the thought off quickly. There won't be years for us. It's just one year. And none of this is real.

Rhodes and his father come barreling through the door, and I can hear they're talking hockey.

"I'm telling you, it's going to be St. Louis you have to watch for this year. They're—" His father stops midsentence, his mouth dropping open as he blinks at me.

I could do the same because I feel like I just met a time traveler. There's no way this isn't just Future Rhodes here to trick me. The two look so alike it's scary.

If Rhodes ages half as well as his father…*damn.*

Rhodes looks from me to his dad and then back again.

I lift my shoulders because I have no idea why Oscar is still staring at me with a look of shock and awe. Or why he's raising his finger and pointing at me.

"Holy shit! You're the alien chick!" *Alien chick?* "Son, why didn't you tell me you were married to the alien girl?"

"I wasn't aware she was an alien." Rhodes looks at me. "How could you not tell me you're an alien? Great! Now the whole marriage is a sham!"

I tuck my lips in, trying hard not to laugh as he smirks at me, enjoying our little inside joke.

"Well, she's not a real alien, but she does her makeup like one."

Wait a minute... "You watch my videos?" I say to Rhodes' father.

He nods enthusiastically. "All the time. Every Tuesday like clockwork. I love the video you did where you transformed into Lady Gaga."

Maggie gasps. "I knew she looked familiar! You're The Beauty Bell!" She looks at her son. "Why didn't you tell us?"

He shrugs. "I wasn't aware you two were avid makeup tutorial connoisseurs."

"Well, you know we were watching that *Drag Race* stuff on the TV, and the way they transform themselves...well, it's hypnotizing! So amazing to watch. We got on YouTube to find some more videos, one thing led to another, and, well, here we are."

My brows shoot up because I am truly and utterly flabbergasted. I was *not* expecting this.

"Oh, you *have* to do one of your looks for us! We want to see the behind-the-scenes magic!" Maggie claps her hands together. "It'll be so fun!"

I inwardly groan. I will definitely have to find a way to get out of that. It's awkward enough filming myself for YouTube sometimes. I can't imagine doing it with an audience.

Rhodes looks at me. "I think my parents are bigger fans of yours than they are of me."

"No," his father says at the same time his mother says, "Yes."

We all laugh.

Maybe this visit won't be so bad after all.

"Oh, for fuck's sake, ref! Open your damn eyes! That wasn't a trip!"

And here I was thinking that based on the way Maggie sobbed during the opening ceremonies as the Comets raised their Stanley Cup Champions banner, she would be the more laid-back one during the game.

I was definitely wrong.

Oscar yanks on Maggie's #6 Rhodes jersey, tugging her back down into her seat. "Now, Maggs, don't be getting yourself all worked up."

Maggie flops back down in her chair, her beer splashing out over the rim of her cup. She shakes her head. "I swear, these refs are just out to get us tonight."

I love how animated Maggie is watching Rhodes fly down the ice. She loves watching her son play hockey, that much is obvious.

I love watching him play too.

I came to several games last season with Harper thanks to Collin hooking us up with tickets, but I never felt as invested in the game as I do now.

Then I cheered on the team.

Now I'm cheering on Rhodes.

"We're still up three–two, and we have a whole other period to play. We got this. I've been watching their goalie and he's getting gassed pretty quick. If they keep shooting top shelf blocker side, they'll be up five–two in no time."

"They've got to stay out of the damn box first," Maggie says.

Honestly, I'm still a little lost on all the logistics of it, but I love watching them play. If you take out all the hitting and punching and a bunch of full-grown men just dogpiling on each other, it's a beautiful game.

Oh, who am I kidding? That part is beautiful too.

And hot. So, *so* hot.

I've been half-horny all night watching Rhodes out on the ice.

He scored a goal earlier, and when he did, he pointed his stick right at me and winked. My panties have been soaked since.

Which is really inconvenient since I'm sitting next to his parents.

"I'm with Maggie on this one, Oscar. These refs are a damn joke tonight," Harper complains, shoving a handful of popcorn in her mouth.

I want to laugh because she's gone from not knowing what a hockey puck was made of to criticizing the refs so fast since she started dating Collin. It's cute how involved she is. Normally, Harper would be in the WAG lounge, which is reserved for the wives and serious girlfriends, but she hates it there and wanted to watch the game with us.

The buzzer sounds as the period comes to an end.

"We're going to grab some boiled peanuts and stretch our legs a bit. Want us to bring you ladies anything back?" Oscar asks, pushing up out of his seat.

I try not to wrinkle my nose at the mention of boiled peanuts, something I could never get into. "Thank you, but I'm okay."

"I'm good too, but thank you," Harper says.

"All right, but if you need anything, just text us, dearies." Maggie pats my shoulder, then shimmies down the aisle to meet up with Oscar.

"So, how's it going with them?" Harper asks once they're out of earshot.

"Good so far. They won't stop giving me suggestions on what character I should turn myself into next, but it's fun still."

"Not awkward at all? You pretending to be married to their son and all that?"

"Actually, no. Not really."

And it's the truth.

I love Rhodes' parents. They're loud, entertaining, and so incredibly sweet. They've welcomed me with open arms, which is more than I could ever ask for.

And really, it's not been hard for Rhodes and me to act like we're married. We've just continued the same routine we've had for the past month.

It's almost as if we actually *are* husband and wife.

"Ryan! Harper!"

I turn toward the voice calling to me and let out a squeal when I see who it is. We rise from our seats and meet our friend Denver halfway down the row.

"Oh gosh, it's so good to see you! What are you doing here?" I ask, hugging her.

"Shep is here schmoozing some people, so I tagged along to get out of the house a bit to escape the chaos of my children." She points up to the suites. "I saw you two from up there and had to come say hi."

Last year I sold some photographs to Denver and her husband, Shep, who happens to be Collin and Rhodes' agent. Us ladies quickly hit it off, and we've stayed connected since. As a gift, Shep gave me tickets to a Comets game. It just happened to be the game where Collin and Harper met.

And I guess where I met Rhodes for the first time too.

I still remember the way he looked at me through the glass after he and Collin crashed into the boards, scaring the shit out of me and Harper. Our eyes locked, and I was in awe. Sure, he had that same scowl he still wears on his face, but it didn't stop me from finding him attractive.

I still do too.

"Anyway," Denver says, "I, uh, heard about your...*situation* with Rhodes." She leans in close. "Don't worry, your secret is safe with me."

"Did Rhodes tell you?"

She lifts her shoulders. "I mean, not officially, but Shep isn't completely clueless. He was able to piece it together when you two went from being nothing to married in a weekend."

I cringe. "It's kind of embarrassing."

"Don't be embarrassed. It happens. Honestly, if you ask me, it sounds like something straight out of a romantic comedy. Who knows? Maybe you'll fall in love for real!"

Love.

The word trips me up.

Sure, things have changed for us since we started sleeping together, but love? No. That's not what this is. It's just two people in an impossible situation making the most of it…right?

I force out a laugh, hoping no one catches on to how fake it sounds.

"Anyway," Denver says, "I just wanted to come down and say hi to you both. I better get back up there though before Shep wonders where I am and goes looking in supply closets for me." I lift my brows, and she waves it off. "Nothing. Inside joke with us." She hugs me again. "It was good seeing you. We should get together for lunch soon."

"That sounds great," I tell her.

"Definitely," Harper agrees.

We make plans to meet up the following week, and she takes off back up the stairs. Luckily, before Harper can make any comments about what Denver said, Maggie and Oscar return. I ignore the hole she's staring into the side of my head as the third period kicks off.

Before I know it, I'm engrossed in the game, forgetting all about Denver's silly fantasy. The Comets take two more penalties—I'm starting to think Maggie was onto something there—and unfortunately, the other team capitalizes on one.

It's down to just three minutes on the clock, and it's tied 3–3. The atmosphere in the arena is tense, everyone hoping the reigning Stanley Cup champions can somehow push ahead and win their first game of the season.

Rhodes is out on the ice. He's holding the puck behind the net, waiting for his team to make a line change. The moment Collin's skates hit the ice, Rhodes takes off. He passes the puck over to Collin, who shoots it back to him.

They drive into the zone and set up the play, playing hot potato with the puck, looking for a way to get it to the net. They're trying to wear the other team down, confuse them. And when Collin fakes the shot, then passes to Rhodes, it works.

He fires a wrister at the net and it sails over the blocker side of the goalie, just like Oscar said they needed to do. The lamp lights up red and the place goes wild, everyone jumping out of their seats cheering—me included.

"BEEEAAASSSTTT!" we all cheer in unison, high-fiving and hugging strangers like we've known each other forever. It's exhilarating.

After it's over, Rhodes is named the first star of the

game and takes a quick interview with the announcer. He looks so uncomfortable during the whole thing, and I know it's because he hates the attention.

The place begins to clear out, and we leave too. We have plans to meet Rhodes and Collin at Slapshots, a local hockey bar, after they're done with their postgame stuff. I guess this is a tradition the guys have.

It doesn't take us long to walk to the bar. Despite the place being crazily packed, we grab a table in the back and order some appetizers and drinks.

Oscar and Maggie are chatting with a few other hockey parents—people they know from attending games over the years—and Harper is deep in discussion with another player's girlfriend about some movie that came out recently.

I don't know how long passes until two arms slip around my waist.

I know instantly it's Rhodes.

"What are you doing out here?" I ask, turning in his arms, looping my arms around his neck. "I figured it would be a while still."

"I always slip out early. Besides, Coach already gave us a speech, and there's no way I'm doing any interviews."

"Not even as the first star of the game?" I grin at him. "You played great, by the way. I'm proud of you."

"Yeah?" He tugs me closer, smiling down at me. "How great we talking here? On a scale of one to I get to see your titties tonight."

"I'd say the chances of it being a titties night are excellent."

"Excellent, huh? Damn, I should have aimed higher. Maybe gone for—"

"If you're even thinking about bringing up what I think you're thinking about, it's a no. Exit only for now."

His smile grows. "For now, huh? Noted."

"God, you're annoying." I try to push from his hold, but he doesn't budge. Instead, he heaves me closer.

"You like it."

"Do not."

He slips his hands into my hair, tilting my head back so I'm looking up at him. "Do too…*wife*."

Then, he kisses me, and that damn four-letter word filters through my mind for the second time tonight.

Love.

Only this time, it doesn't trip me up nearly as much, and I don't know how to feel about that.

"Don't forget, I like my wieners—"

"Long and thick? Oh, I am *well* aware, Maggs." Oscar bounces his brows up and down at his wife.

"Well, yes." Maggie blushes. "But you know I meant well done, Oscar." She slaps at him playfully.

I glance over at Rhodes, who looks like he's about to vomit.

"I think your father is talking about his dick."

Rhodes glares at me. "Shut—and I mean this respectfully—the fuck up."

I laugh. "Oh, lighten up. Your parents have seen each other's naughty bits. They've even had sex, Rhodes."

"I want a divorce."

I lift a brow. "Really, now?" I hold my left hand up and pinch my thumb and forefinger around my wedding band, tugging it up. "Because I'll—"

He points the tongs he's holding at me. "Don't you fucking dare take that off."

A shiver runs through me at the low growl in his words.

I've come to learn that Rhodes *really* likes the look of a ring on my finger, and I have to admit, seeing him all riled up about it does something to me I can't explain.

It makes me feel good, desired…and confused.

I push that part away.

"I'm going to go check on the macaroni. Try not to let visions of humping and grinding and your par—"

"Ryan Bell!"

I cackle at the way his face reddens, then quickly slam the back door closed as he charges at me.

The door slides open shortly after, Maggie following me into the kitchen.

"Would you like some help?" she asks as I pull open the oven to check on the food. "I'm great in the kitchen."

"Sure. Can you grab the toppings from the fridge and get them settled on the platter? The macaroni is nearly finished. Just need to let it broil a bit longer."

"Of course."

She busies herself gathering the toppings from the fridge and arranging them like they're being photographed for some fancy food magazine.

I stop in front of the kitchen sink to wash my hands so I can help, when from the corner of my eye I catch Rhodes outside.

His head is thrown back in a laugh over something his father said, and he looks so…free. I've noticed that about him recently. How his smiles are coming easier, and his shoulders aren't as weighed down by that invisible weight he seems to carry. I've even noticed that he full-on laughs at least twice a day now. A feat for him, really.

It's…beautiful. *He's* beautiful.

And right now, in this moment, with the sunlight hitting just behind him, he looks picturesque.

My hands ache for the weight of my camera to catch this moment.

"The way you look at him…" Maggie's words draw my attention. "It's…well, it reminds me of Oscar and myself."

A twinge of guilt hits me, her comparing our fake marriage to their very real one.

"It does?"

"Yes. The way you love him is clear as day, and I have to say… I'm so happy. I'm so happy because I was so worried he wouldn't ever find this kind of love. Not because he doesn't deserve it or because of that damn scar that changed his life. But because I was scared he wouldn't *allow* himself to be loved like this. With you, I don't have that worry. He's finally back to…well, himself."

I wasn't expecting her to say that. And I really wasn't expecting the burn at the back of my throat.

I swallow, trying to find words. Any words.

But nothing comes.

She rests her hand on my forearm as I blink back the tears stinging my eyes. "I'm so glad you've found each other, Ryan. You're good for him, and something tells me he's good for you too."

Something tells me…she's right.

CHAPTER 17

RYAN & RHODES

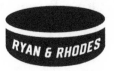

Ryan: Please don't be mad at me.

Rhodes: Absolutely nothing good ever follows that.

Ryan: I need you to promise.

Rhodes: No.

Ryan: No you won't be mad or no you're not going to promise?

Rhodes: Just no. Whatever it is, no.

. . .

Rhodes: Okay, fine. Tell me. I'm curious.

Ryan: Well now I DON'T want to tell you because you're going to be mad.

Rhodes: Just tell me.

Ryan: Nah.

Rhodes: Ryan…

Rhodes: Tell me.

Ryan: Or?

Rhodes: Or?

Rhodes: What do you mean OR?

. . .

Ryan: Tell you OR what? What are you going to do if I don't tell you?

Ryan: Fly here?

Rhodes: YES. And spank you.

Rhodes: Except not in a fun way this time.

Ryan: It's always a fun way. *smirk emoji*

Rhodes: Have I…unlocked a hidden kink?

Ryan: I'm not sure. We may have to test it more.

Rhodes: *warms palm up*

Rhodes: WAIT.

Rhodes: No.

. . .

Rhodes: Tell me what you were going to tell me.

Ryan: Nah.

Rhodes: Yes.

Ryan: No.

Rhodes: Don't make me book a flight.

Ryan: You wouldn't.

Rhodes: You're right. I'll just worry the whole night and play an awful game and that will be on YOUR shoulders.

Ryan: Wow. So that's how you're going to play it, huh?

Rhodes: Exactly like that.

. . .

Rhodes: Ryan?

Rhodes: RYAN?

Rhodes: Fine. But if I lose tonight, know it's your fault.

Ryan: Okay, wow. That's just mean.

Ryan: Poe puked in your bed.

Rhodes: Oh. Is that it?

Ryan: And your closet.

Rhodes: Oh.

Ryan: And in your shoes.

Rhodes: Which ones???

. . .

Ryan: And maybe on your couch too.

Rhodes: WTF

Rhodes: Okay, okay. It's fine. No biggie.

Rhodes: What's wrong with her?

Ryan: I took her to the vet and apparently she's eating too fast. I think she's scared Frodo is going to eat all her food, so she's gobbling it down.

Rhodes: But they're getting along so well.

Ryan: I know. But cats are weird.

Rhodes: Well, her throwing up on everything is fine. I'm not mad.

Ryan: So then you won't be mad if I also tell you I spilled red wine on the couch?

. . .

Rhodes: ...

Rhodes: You're going to be the death of me.

Ryan: Am not. I'm cute.

Rhodes: And a pain in my ass.

Rhodes: I need to get ready.

Ryan: GO TEAM GO!

Rhodes: Death of me.

Ryan: You were so close on that goal! That ping off the crossbar was LOUD!

. . .

Ryan: Ugh. Fuck New York. That hit was bullshit. Totally dirty.

Ryan: Oh my god. You have to be kidding me?! They called THAT a trip??

Ryan: HOLY SHIT YOU SCORED!!

Ryan: Great. Now I'm wet.

Ryan: Ugh. Why does hockey make me so horny???

Ryan: Hmmm…maybe I should have gotten a new sex toy.

Rhodes: Okay, wow. We need to lay down a few ground rules.

Rhodes: #1: You CANNOT tell me you're horny and wet when I'm hundreds of miles away. Well, you can, but only when I'm able to FaceTime you or something so we can take care of it together.

. . .

Rhodes: #2: If you're getting new toys, I want to help pick them out. That way when you're using them, you'll think of me.

Ryan: I'd think of you anyway.

Rhodes: Hm. If I didn't know any better, I'd say you're starting to like me.

Ryan: Your dick. I'm starting to like your dick.

Rhodes: It is a great dick.

Ryan: Yeah? I heard it was a burden. Too big to carry around.

Rhodes: Just the cross I have to bear.

Ryan: You're exhausting.

. . .

Ryan: Good game tonight, btw. You did amazing.

Rhodes: Thank you.

Rhodes: I…I like it when you watch my games.

Ryan: Yeah? Guess I'll have to keep watching then.

Rhodes: You're only saying that because they make you horny.

Rhodes: Wait. Are you still horny? Did you…take care of yourself during the game?

Ryan: …

Rhodes: Oh fuck. You did, didn't you?

Ryan: *zips lips*

. . .

Rhodes: Holy hell. I'll be at the hotel in ten minutes. You'd better answer my call.

Ryan: Sorry tonight didn't go good for you guys.

Rhodes: It happens. Had to break the winning streak at some point.

Ryan: *picture*

Ryan: This should make you feel better. They've been curled up like that together for the last hour.

Rhodes: That does make me feel a little better.

Ryan: I'm still surprised they're getting along so well. Poe is a moody bitch half the time. Harper thinks it's funny because Poe is grumpy and I'm not, and you're grumpy and Frodo is the sweetest thing in the world. She thinks we adopted the wrong pets.

. . .

Rhodes: Harper may be onto something.

Ryan: I'm not telling her that. She'll gloat too much.

Ryan: She says hi, btw.

Rhodes: Is she there?

Ryan: Yes. That's okay, right?

Rhodes: Of course. It's your place too.

Ryan: Does that mean I can hang some photos around here? I was teasing about the castle thing, but I'm starting to suspect I was right…

Rhodes: Go for it.

Ryan: Really???

. . .

Rhodes: Were you expecting a different answer?

Ryan: Honestly, yes.

Ryan: But I'm not about to look a gift horse in the mouth.

Rhodes: I do have a stipulation.

Ryan: Naturally.

Rhodes: It has to be your photos.

Ryan: I think I can manage that.

Rhodes: The bus to the hotel is leaving soon. Call you when I get there?

Ryan: Yes.

. . .

Rhodes: You should probably tell Harper to leave.

Ryan: Why?

Rhodes: Because I want to see you.

Ryan: Okay…

Rhodes: All of you.

Ryan: Oh. OH.

Ryan: Consider it done.

Rhodes: And Ryan?

Ryan: Yes?

Rhodes: That new toy you got?

. . .

Rhodes: Have it ready.

Ryan: *picture*

Ryan: Grams loves her jersey! She says thank you!

Rhodes: Anything to get her to stop wearing Collin's number.

Ryan: Oh, she still has that. It was under her pillow earlier when I left.

Rhodes: I don't get it. He's not even that great.

Rhodes: I lied. He's the most amazing defenseman on the team. Definitely the best.

Rhodes: Most handsome too.

Ryan: Hi Collin.

. . .

Rhodes: Hey Ryan. Your husband is a grump. You should send him more pictures of

Rhodes: Okay, wow. Ignore him. He's an idiot.

Ryan: Now I'm curious what I need to send you more pictures of.

Rhodes: Nothing.

Rhodes: Though I wouldn't complain about some sexy photos…

Ryan: I am not sending you nudes.

Rhodes: I never said anything about being nude.

Rhodes: I'm kidding anyway. You don't need to send me photos.

. . .

Ryan: *picture*

Rhodes: HOLY FUCK

Rhodes: Is that…? In my jersey??

Rhodes: You're seriously killing me right now. I still have to catch a flight home.

Ryan: You should probably hurry up then.

Rhodes: Ryan?

Ryan: Yeah?

Rhodes: I expect you to be wearing that when I get home.

Ryan: Yes, husband.

CHAPTER 18

RHODES

I can't remember a time when I was ever this eager to get a game over with.

We've been on the road for the last week, and all I want to do is crawl into my bed and wrap my arms around Ryan for a week straight.

Obviously, that week-straight part won't happen, but still. I just want to be at home.

It has nothing to do with hockey either. We're currently 9—2—1. We're playing like the champions we are, and my numbers are looking damn good. I've put up four goals and five assists. I've never started a season this hot before. I feel good on the ice. My playing is at its all-time best. I feel rested and relaxed, and I'm making good plays.

So why am I eager to get home and away from the game I love so much?

Ryan.

The more time we spend together, the more I hate leaving her for these road games, which is crazy to me. I love hockey. I've always loved hockey. It's been my life for as long as I can remember. It's always been an escape, and even more so after my accident. I was able to lose myself in the game and ignore the rest.

But lately, I don't want to escape. I just want to spend time with Ryan.

I'll admit, when Collin and Harper started dating, I did my best to avoid her. It pissed me off how easily she charmed everyone around her. It was easy for her to command the attention of any group because of her beauty, and frankly, it annoyed me.

But what I know now is I was missing all those special parts of her that she keeps hidden under the surface. She's more than the bubbly, sunshiny personality she puts out there. She's deep and thoughtful and just a touch emotionally scarred from her parents leaving her. But she's also funny, and smart, and caring. The way she gives everything up for the people she loves most in her life blows me away.

She blows me away.

My phone buzzes on the bench next to me and I pick it up. I don't typically spend time on my phone before games, but when I see Ryan's name come across my screen, I can't help but snatch it.

And I'm glad I did.

Ryan: *picture*

. . .

Ryan: Good luck! We're rooting for you!!

She looks so fucking cute sitting there in my jersey, Poe and Frodo flanking her on the couch.

She's been doing this every night I've been away, sending me little *good luck* texts or congratulations afterward. Sometimes she'll even text me play-by-plays as she sees them from a different angle.

It's cute as hell, and I look forward to them way more than I'd like to admit.

"Dude, based on the way you're looking at that phone right now, I'd say you just got a very nice picture from your lady," Collin says, flopping down on the bench next to me.

"You sound like Miller."

Collin's face twists up. "Oh, fuck. I do. Gross."

"Hey! I heard that," Miller says, flipping us off.

"Sorry. I think I'm just horny."

Now it's my turn to look disgusted. "I'd really rather not hear about your dick problems, thank you."

"I'm just saying, being away this long fucking blows. One more game and I get to go home to my girl."

"I hear you there."

I know the moment I say it, I'm about to catch hell.

"Oh, you hear me, huh?"

I sigh. "Don't you have someone else to go bother?"

"And miss that annoyed scowl on your face? No, thanks."

Said scowl deepens, and he laughs.

"I take it things are still going well?" I nod. "You two have been looking awfully cozy lately."

"Is that a bad thing?"

"No. Just…"

When he doesn't continue, I lift my hands. "Just what?"

"I don't know. Be careful, I guess."

"Be careful?"

He nods. "Yeah. You know…because of the whole 'faking it' thing."

I glance around the room, but nobody is paying us any attention.

"There's nothing to worry about. We've drawn some pretty clear lines."

He studies me. "Have you?"

"Yeah."

"So you definitely have boundaries, then?"

"For sure."

"And you're following them?"

"Mostly, yeah."

"Mostly?"

"She has her own bedroom."

He doesn't look impressed. "Does she sleep in there?"

I don't answer that, which is answer enough.

"See my point? You're already breaking all your rules, even the simple ones. You have to keep things separate or else it's going to start feeling real."

I gulp.

Things already feel real.

"Oh. Okay. Wow. Disregard everything I just said." He waves a hand in front of my face. "It's clear as day I'm too late."

"Huh?"

Collin's brows are near his hairline, and he's looking at me like I'm stupid. "You're in love with her, dude."

I scoff, rolling my eyes. "I am not."

"You are. You really are."

"I'm really not. I promise."

"Uh-huh. So she's not the first thing you think about in the mornings?"

"Well, yeah, but only because she's usually stolen all the covers in the middle of the night and I'm annoyed with her."

"Hm. Okay. She's not the person you're most excited to see when you get home from an away game?"

"Frodo is."

"Right. And she's definitely not the one who has you acting like an actual human for once and not walking around like you have a stick up your ass?"

"She…" Well, okay. So I *have* been more… approachable lately. But that's just because I've been getting laid regularly, I'm sure. "No. It's not like that."

Collin chuckles. "Right. Sure. Whatever you have to keep telling yourself."

"I'm not *telling* myself anything. It's true."

"Okay."

I scrub a hand down my face, my irritation growing. "Stop doing that."

"Doing what?"

"Saying okay like that—like you don't believe me."

"I'm not saying I don't believe you. I'm just saying you're full of shit."

"Collin..."

"Rhodes..." he mocks. "Look, I'm just saying, would it really be such a bad thing if you were in love with her? I mean, she *is* your wife after all."

Would it be a bad thing if I were in love with Ryan? Yes, yes it would be.

And that's because she's my wife but not my *wife*. We're married, but only on paper. It's not like she's with me because she actually likes me. If we hadn't gotten drunk married, we would have continued on ignoring one another just like we were. There'd be no *this* right now.

So, can I be in love with her? No.

Collin pats me on the back, then pushes up off the bench. "Just be careful," he repeats. "And get those fucking skates on. We got a game to win."

The house is dark when I get home. I stop in the kitchen for a quick bottle of water and then check to make sure Frodo and Poe are comfortable. They're in their now usual position of being snuggled together in Frodo's bed.

I step into the bedroom and marvel at the sight in front of me.

Ryan is curled up in the middle—because that's where she always sleeps—and she has her arms wrapped around *my* pillow. The moonlight is filtering over her, the light and shadows mixed to create a stunning image.

I'm not good with the camera, but I grab hers anyway and snap a quick picture. It'll be a surprise for her when she wakes. I set the camera on the bedside table and almost feel bad about having to crawl into bed with her because she looks so peaceful.

But I can't *not* touch her right now.

I strip my clothes off, tossing them haphazardly across the room, and climb into bed behind her. I wrap my arm around her waist, tugging her close. There's no way she doesn't feel my hard cock against her bare ass.

I know it too because it doesn't take long before she's wiggling against me, stirring awake. She tangles our fingers together, and I rub at her ring.

"Hey," she mutters, her voice scratchy and full of sleep. "I tried waiting up for you, but I passed out." She rolls over in my arms, facing me. "That was an intense game, but I'm glad you guys won."

"I'm glad we did too."

New York ended up scoring with just a minute left in the third period. Overtime was fucking exhausting, and neither team could capitalize on it. We finally won in the shootout with a wicked rocket from Miller. Fucking rookie saved our asses again. He'll never let us live it down.

"I missed you," I say to her, capturing her mouth for a kiss.

I fit my lips against hers and kiss her lazily, taking my time as our tongues stroke together.

She grins against me when I finally pull away. "I missed you too."

"Yeah?"

"On a scale of one to seeing my titties..." she says, pushing me onto my back. She climbs on top of me, straddling me just like she did that first morning. "It's a solid titties."

She grabs the hem of her shirt, ready to strip it off, but I stop her.

"Wait." Her brows scrunch together. "Leave it on."

"On? But I thought..."

I tug her down, kissing her quickly. "I'd love to see your titties, baby girl, but right now, what I'd love even more is to eat your pussy while you sit on my face wearing my jersey."

Her eyes gloss over at my words, and I know she wants that too.

I smack at her ass. "Get up there."

She moves faster than I've ever seen her move before, fitting her knees around my head.

"Hands on the headboard, Ryan."

She tugs her bottom lip between her teeth and does what I say.

"Lower."

"Huh?"

"Lower. Sit lower."

"But…"

"I said sit, not hover." I smack her ass again and she moans. "Lower."

She obliges, lowering her pussy to my mouth.

She sighs the moment my tongue slides against her, her eyes rolling back in her head. And I do as I promise. I tongue-fuck her cunt and suck her clit into my mouth. I eat her, taking my time to get my fill so long that she stops being worried about suffocating me and starts fucking herself on my face.

I feel her trembling from the exhaustion of holding herself up, and I know she's teetering closer and closer to the edge by the second.

I test my luck by sliding my finger through her wet folds, back to her hole. She tenses when my finger brushes against her. I suck her clit into my mouth again, playing with her until she relaxes against the touch.

"Rhodes…" She whimpers when I slip the tip of my finger in.

I keep my mouth on her, not letting up, and it's not long before she's rocking against it, pushing my digit in deeper.

And it's not long after that until she's coming apart.

I withdraw my finger as her shakes subside, continuing to lap at her until she comes down off her high. She scoots back down my body looking satiated—but I'm not done with her yet.

I flip her onto her back, fitting myself between her legs and sliding into her without hesitation.

"*Ooohh,*" she cries out, arching into me as I fuck into her slowly.

I cradle her face in my hands, kissing her, letting the strokes of my tongue match what I'm doing between her legs.

It's a slow, agonizing dance and I want to fuck her harder and faster, but I want to take my time too.

Her breaths begin coming in sharper, and I know another orgasm is building.

"Rhodes…I need…"

She doesn't have to finish her sentence. I know her body by heart at this point.

I push to my knees, keeping my slow, languid pace, and press my thumb to her clit. She sighs at my touch, panting and pleading for a release.

Finally, she breaks, spasming around me, milking my own orgasm from my body.

Exhausted, I collapse, rolling onto my back and taking her with me. She's sprawled across me, her body limp and worn.

"So good. So, so good," she murmurs, the words slurred with sleep.

It's not long before I hear the faint sounds of her snoring.

I don't know how long I lie there watching her, her head resting on my chest, her features soft and sated.

But I do know she's perfect. *This* is perfect. Nothing in the world could be better than this moment.

And that's what scares me the most.

CHAPTER 19

RYAN

"Oh god. *Oooooh.* Fucking hell. *Oh.*"

"Um, can you please stop moaning like that? Pretty sure you're making everyone uncomfortable right now."

Collin points to his lap. "Especially my dick because these are new jeans, and I haven't stretched them out properly yet so there's like nowhere for my boner to go."

"Collin!" Harper's eyes widen. "Good grief. What is wrong with you?"

"Me? What's wrong with you?! You're the one moaning over here like you were last night when I—"

She slaps a hand over his mouth. "Do not finish that sentence." She gives him a warning look, then removes her hand. "Sorry. These donuts are just seriously *so* good."

It's true. These donuts are really good.

"I had no idea this place even existed. I feel like I've been missing out."

I glance around the lot the adorable little baby blue food truck is in. There are a few picnic tables spread around and a small coffee bar off to the right of the truck. There is a line at least five people deep, and it's been consistently busy since we got here.

How I didn't have a clue about this place, I don't know.

"You have been. It's seriously so good. I'm addicted."

"Well, if *someone*"—I look pointedly at Rhodes—"would have told me about it before, I could have been eating donuts every day."

He holds his hands up innocently. "Hey, I tried bringing you before my last home game, but *no*. You had a video to film and wouldn't let me in the room for some reason."

"Ugh. This again?" I roll my eyes. "Harper, will you please tell Rhodes here I do not have to let him sit in on me making my makeup tutorials?"

"Oh, one hundred percent no. You do not have to allow him in there. I don't allow Collin in my studio even though he asks me all the time."

"Like all the fucking time, and she just won't let me in. I don't get it."

"Because it's *my* studio. I don't ask you to go out on the hockey rink and do hockey things, now do I? No, because that's *your* space."

"I'll take you skating. I'll take you skating right fucking now. Get some skates on. Let's go," Collin says, rising from the bench we're currently sitting on.

Harper grabs his jacket, pulling him back down. "Oh my god. Shut up, sit down, and eat your damn donuts."

I turn to Rhodes, satisfied with Harper's answer. "See, I told you it's not weird that I won't let you watch."

"Okay, now that sounds a little dirty. What kind of videos? I'd watch." Collin bounces his brows up and down. Harper smacks him in the back of the head. "Wow. Geez, I was kidding."

"Fine," Rhodes says. "I get it. It's your space. It's your thing. I don't need to be there all up in your business. But I do think it's pretty fucking cool."

"So cool. I had no idea so many steps and so much time and products were involved. I can't believe the way people can transform their faces with just makeup." He turns to Harper. "Maybe you should do that, start doing your makeup more often."

Harper, who is completely engrossed in her donuts, does the slowest, creepiest turn I've ever seen. Her eyes are dark and dangerous, and her eyebrows are about up to her hairline as she looks to her boyfriend. "Excuse me? Did you just tell me I need to wear more makeup?"

At first, Collin looks confused.

Then, it hits him, and he nearly jumps off the bench.

"What, no? No, no, no! I was just saying, you know, because she does like fun, crazy, cool stuff. I thought you could do fun, crazy, cool stuff too, but scary. Because you love scary and scary things make you happy and I love when you're happy and definitely don't want to murder me."

He's talking a mile a minute trying to correct his

mistake, but it's no use. Harper's already off the bench and ready to pounce.

I have to give Collin credit. He is a lot smarter than I thought because he takes off at a dead sprint, running from his girlfriend who is now chasing after him.

Rhodes and I fall into a fit of laughter watching Harper trying to catch up to him.

"Well, he really botched that one, didn't he?"

"Afraid so," Rhodes says. "And to think he was going to propose to her today."

I gasp. "Was he really?"

"Oh fuck." Rhodes drops his head into his hands. "I wasn't supposed to say anything. But, yeah, he's planning to propose."

"How? What does he—" I gasp again. "Wait…he asked me for the footage from my exhibit and Harper said something about them going out to some old horror movie at that ancient theater downtown tonight. Is he doing it there?"

"He is. I have no idea on the specifics, but he has this whole thing planned."

"Is the ring pretty?"

"Very. I'm actually surprised he didn't go to you about it."

"Me too. I have great taste. But I totally would have slipped and told Harper, so it's probably a good thing he didn't. I'm awful at keeping secrets."

"You're keeping our secret pretty well."

"Yeah, but this is easy."

A look crosses his face that I can't quite decipher, but it doesn't necessarily make me feel bad. His mouth drops open like he's going to say something, but he thinks better of it, snapping it shut and shaking his head.

"What?" I ask.

"It's nothing. I just—"

Harper flops down on the bench across from us, interrupting whatever he was going to say with her harsh breaths.

Rhodes looks away, clearing his throat. "Did you lose him?"

"Nope, he's up a tree."

"A tree."

"Yep. The coward literally climbed a tree to avoid my wrath."

"Oh god." Rhodes groans and stands up. "I'll go get him down." He ambles away in search of his friend.

"Did I just interrupt something? It looked like whatever you two were talking about was pretty intense."

I wave her off. "Nah. I'm sure it was nothing."

Except it didn't feel like nothing.

It felt like something. Something big.

"Okay, *puh-lease* tell me I'm seeing what I think I'm seeing right now."

A woman stands at the end of the table looking at the opposite side of the parking lot where Rhodes is trying to coax Collin out of the tree.

"Unfortunately, that is exactly what it looks like," Harper confirms for her.

"I…wow. And to think, those are professional athletes."

"Underneath all that hockey player bravado, they're boys. And we all know—"

"Boys are dumb," we all three say at the same time.

We burst into giggles.

The woman takes a seat next to Harper, then sticks her hand out to me. "I don't think we've met yet. I'm Scout, the owner and resident baker."

"*You're* the brilliant woman behind these amazing donuts?"

She nods as I slide my hand into hers. "The one and only."

"I'm Ryan, Rhodes' wife."

"Oh, I'm aware. Those headlines were…*wow*. I don't know how you do it. I'd die being in the spotlight like that." She shudders. "But congratulations on the marriage. You two look so happy and in love."

Harper and I exchange a look, trying to hold back our laughter.

"Thank you. It was a whirlwind romance, that's for sure."

Scout sighs dreamily, dropping her chin into her hand. "Romance…that sounds so nice. And so far out of reach."

"Trust me, it is not all it's cracked up to be. Case in point"—Harper points to where Rhodes is still trying to get Collin down—"that."

Scout twists her lips up. "Point taken. I just wish…

ugh, never mind. Ignore me. Just the mindless ramblings of a woman who is perpetually single and sad because she's an aspiring romance novelist who has never been in love."

"You write romance?" I perk up, excited because *love*.

"I dabble. A dream, really, you know?"

"I'd love to read what you have. I'm a huge sucker for all things romance."

"It's true. It's annoying."

"Oh, pipe down over there. You can't be against love when you're in it."

Harper grins, not looking the least bit sorry.

"What kind of romance novel?"

"It's an unrequited love story. Mostly because that's all I know." She shrugs. "Anyway, it's definitely not ready for reading, but maybe once I get it finished?"

"Yes!"

"Will there be bloody, gruesome murders or scary serial killers in it?" Harper asks.

"No."

"Boo. Then count me out."

Scout laughs, rising from the table and brushing the backs of her pants off. "All right, well, back to work. I just had to come over and say hi and introduce myself." She turns to Harper. "As always, so good to see you."

"Now that we've initiated Ryan into our little secret donut club, we'll have to stop by more often."

"Please do." Scout beams at me. "Congratulations again on the recent nuptials. The way he looks at you is…well, it's what romance novels are based on." She backs away with a wave and a smile.

"I like her. She seems sweet," I say to Harper once we're alone again.

"Very sweet and shy. She seems to be doing an amazing job with this place. It's been packed every time I've been here."

"Impressive."

Harper nods. "So, speaking of cute together…how are things with you and Rhodes? Is everything still going okay?"

"Yeah, actually. Everything is…well, really great."

And it's the truth. Things have been going so well lately. Scary well. And not just things with Rhodes and me either.

My grams is happy and thriving at her new assisted living facility. She loves her suitemate and all the nurses. She's taking part in more group activities than she ever did before.

My YouTube channel has grown by twenty thousand subscribers in the last month, which means more views, which in turn means more profit. I'm not dumb—I know a lot of that has to do with marrying Rhodes and people being curious about our relationship, but I'm not about to look a gift horse in the mouth.

I've kept true to his request to not post about us, but Poe and Frodo have become fixtures on my Instagram page.

"Good, I'm glad. I won't lie, I was a little worried about you two."

"Worried?"

"Yeah. I mean, you're just *so* different. He's like this total reclusive grump and you're always the life of the party. I wasn't sure how that would work out. But now…" She trails off and then shrugs. "I don't know. This might be *way* off base and totally crazy, but Scout was right—he does look at you like something straight out of a book. It almost seems like you guys aren't pretending anymore."

My initial instinct is to refute her claims because that's not true. Of course we're still pretending.

But…

"I…I'm not so sure I am pretending anymore."

"Are you saying…"

"I think I'm in love with my fake husband."

I take a step back, admiring my work hanging on the gallery wall.

Somehow, and I have no idea how I got so lucky, Rhodes gave me permission to use some shots from our session together.

I was nervous to approach him about it and fully expected him to tell me no, but he didn't. In fact, he called it my best work to date and encouraged it.

I've been teasing him about being a "model" ever since.

"It's breathtaking."

I glance over at the gentleman standing next to me. He's older than me by several years, wearing a button-up long-sleeve shirt that's rolled to his elbows and a pair of dark gray slacks. Tattoos cover his forearms, making him look younger.

He's handsome…and totally married.

A blush steals up my cheeks at his compliment. "Thank you."

"The raw emotion you captured is just…*wow.*" He gives his head a small shake, eyes wide with amazement as he stares up at the photo. "That's Adrian Rhodes from the Carolina Comets, right?"

"It is. Are you a Comets fan?"

"Huge. I don't make it out to as many games as I like, but I never miss one on TV." He pulls his hand from his pocket and sticks it out to me. "I'm Winston Daniels. By the way, big fan of your work."

"Of my…photography?" I ask, shaking his hand.

"Yeah. You sound surprised by that though."

I shrug. "Sorry, I just always assume if people know me, it's from my—"

"Makeup tutorials? My twin sister, Wren, is a big fan of *that* work of yours."

"Oh." I laugh. "Thank you. Are you a photographer too?"

"I am. I mostly specialize in weddings and family

portraits, but whenever I can, I get out and grab some nature shots too."

"Oh!" Recognition dawns on me. "You're *that* Winston Daniels. I saw your photo of the wave that went viral, and I went down a rabbit hole of your work. It's amazing, the way you can capture nature like that."

He nods toward the photograph we're standing in front of. "Same could be said for the way you capture emotion. I swear, I can *feel* his pain just by looking at this photo."

"It was an intense session, that's for sure." I try my damnedest not to blush remembering what happened at the end of said session. "What brings you out here tonight?"

The gallery I hold my exhibits in downtown is having a showing tonight for local artists. Rhodes is currently on a long stretch of away games, and Harper is visiting her mother and sister on the other side of the state to celebrate her engagement. Collin *did* propose, and I am over the moon for them.

"My wife and I are here celebrating our anniversary. She's around here somewhere. She's not really big into photography, so I'm sure she's back there hanging out in the corner where all the nude portraits are."

"Hey, I've seen some of those. Not a bad corner to be in."

He laughs. "Well, I don't want to take up any more of your time. I just wanted to say, photographer to photographer, your work is amazing."

I blush again. "Thank you. I truly do appreciate the compliment."

"And please, tell your husband good luck in his game tomorrow night. I can't believe I'm about to say this, but I would love to see the Comets whoop some St. Louis ass tomorrow."

"I will definitely pass on the message. It was great to meet you, Winston."

"Likewise, Ryan."

With a small wave, he disappears into the crowd.

I turn back to the photo of my husband. Longing pulls at my chest.

I miss him. So much more than I thought I would.

I didn't realize how lonely it could be to be the wife of a pro hockey player. They're gone all the time, and when they are home, they spend a lot of time at the rink practicing and the games go late into the night.

It's tough, and I don't think I ever gave Harper enough credit for having to deal with this all the time.

"I'm surprised he allowed you to put that ugly thing on display."

I am so taken aback by the words that it takes me a moment to realize the person who said them is speaking to me.

I turn to my left, and I don't even have to ask who the woman standing there is because I already know.

She huffs, flipping her hair over her shoulder. "God, look at him crying. What a baby. *Oh, boohoo, poor me I have a scar on my face; everybody feel bad for me.* Please, he's like a gazillionaire. How can you be sad when you have money?"

My blood boils at her words, and I have to work overtime to keep my cool.

Don't hit her, don't hit her, don't hit her. She's not worth it. Do not hit her.

I have never punched somebody in my life, but I really want to fucking hit her.

"What are you doing here, Brittney?"

"Oh, so you know who I am. Guess that means Rhodes talks about me, huh?"

"No. Actually, he hasn't mentioned you. The subject of trolls doesn't really come up all that often."

She narrows her eyes at me, her face pinched tight. "Right. Sure."

"I'll ask you again, what are you doing here? You have no business being here."

"I just had to see for myself if the rumors were true and Adrian actually is married to some little wannabe social media star. With the lack of photos on your Instagram, I was beginning to think it was all a publicity stunt."

I give her a tight-lipped smile. "Nope. We are definitely married. But thanks for being a follower."

She glances down at the simple gold wedding band I have around my finger, seeming rather unimpressed by it. "Right, and you expect me to believe Adrian Rhodes bought you that wedding ring? I doubt that."

"Doubt it all you want, but we have the marriage certificate to prove it."

That's not actually true. I haven't yet seen a copy of the certificate.

But I know it's real. I was there.

I don't need to prove my marriage to anyone, let alone the woman who stomped on Rhodes' heart.

"You know, I—"

I hold my hand up, stopping her. "Save it. I don't care what you have to say about anything. I have no idea what your real motive is for being here, but I don't have the patience to deal with your ass."

She snaps her mouth shut, her fists balling at her sides. "You *bitch*."

I snort. "Trust me, I've been called worse." I take a step toward her, not missing the way she flinches. "Just to set the record straight"—I point at the photo of Rhodes—"there is *nothing* ugly about that man—my *husband*—and you were goddamn lucky to have him for the time you did. But that's over and done, and so are you. I'm going to give you one last chance to walk out of here before I drag you into the street like the trash you are."

She stands there, eyes wide, stunned.

And frankly, I'm stunned too, but mostly because I mean the words.

She pushes her tits out, shoving her shoulders back. "Fine, I'm leaving. But this isn't over."

"Oh, but it is."

And I walk away from her barely holding it together.

CHAPTER 20

RHODES

I am fuming.

It's been a few days since Ryan told me about the incident with Brittney, and I'm still pissed about it. I immediately tried to call her, but even though she's been calling me nonstop since Vegas, she didn't answer. I tried Colter too, and like the coward he is, I got no response.

I think the part that pisses me off the most is that I couldn't be there to protect her from Brittney's bullshit.

"Dude, you good?" Collin asks from the stationary bike next to me. "You look like you're pushing it way harder than normal."

"I'm fine." But the words don't even sound fine to my ears.

"Everything good with you and Ryan?"

"No. Well, yes. But no."

"Okay, totally not confusing at all."

I slow my pedaling down. I'm an idiot. Yeah, I'm pissed the fuck off, but I don't need to punish my body for it. Especially not when we have a game tonight and I need the rest.

I'm just so fucking worked up that I *need* to release some of this pent-up energy.

"Sorry, man," I say, wiping the sweat off my forehead. "There was an incident with Brittney while we were in San Jose."

"What?" He slows his own bike down. "What the hell happened?"

"I don't know. I guess Brittney accosted Ryan when she was at the gallery downtown. Came in talking about how she wanted to make sure we were actually married or some shit. Who fucking knows? She's clearly off her rocker."

"Dude, she's always been off her rocker. The way she's played you with that back-and-forth game…she's got issues, man."

"I know. I know I should have listened to you. I know that now. Maybe if I had, I wouldn't be in this situation right now."

"Yeah, but maybe the situation isn't so bad anymore. I mean with you being madly in love with your wife and all."

He looks surprised when I don't start immediately refuting his claim.

"What? Not going to try to tell me otherwise?"

I shrug. "I don't know. Getting kind of tired of trying to convince myself it's not true."

He grins. "Fucking knew it. You're in *looooove*."

"Shut up," I grumble, but there's no bite behind it.

"You hear that, boys?" Collin shouts loudly. "Our boy is in love!"

"Yeah, no fucking shit. He's married," Miller says back.

"About damn time," Lowell mutters.

Collin pats me on the back, and I shrug his hand off. "Stop making it weird, dude. It's not that big of a deal."

"Not that big of a deal? You're known for being emotionally unavailable. This is a *huge* deal."

I guess he's right. I am pretty emotionally closed off most of the time. But it's kind of hard not to be when you're me. Shit, look at what happened with Brittney. I took a chance with a girl and made myself vulnerable for the first time in a long time, and where did it get me? I got my heart stomped on.

I realize now what I had with her wasn't love, and I know that because whatever I felt for her pales in comparison to what I feel for Ryan.

With Ryan, it's this carnal need for her all the time, and not just in a sexual way. I miss her constantly, sometimes even when she's sitting right next to me. All I want to do is be around her and be with her. I want to celebrate her milestones and her good news, and I want to experience all her downs too.

I never had that with Brittney. Hell, there were some days I couldn't even stand to be around her. But I settled. I settled because I thought that was all I deserved.

I was so fucking wrong.

Collin hops off the stationary bike, grabbing a towel and wiping his face off. "I'm happy for you, man. Look at us couple of saps in love. Who would have thought?"

Not me, that's for damn sure.

"I'm going to hit the showers and then get home to grab a nap before the game. And by nap, I mean I'm probably going to snuggle with Harper and the dogs on the couch. Can you believe that woman doesn't like naps? Who doesn't nap? Psychos, that's who."

Definitely psychos. "I'm going to do a few more miles and then head home myself. I'll catch you at the game tonight."

"All right, man. Sounds good." We bump our knuckles together and he disappears out the door.

I keep going, pushing myself for another three miles. By the time I'm finished, Lowell and Miller have already gone home too, and it's just me left.

I hit the showers, enjoying the hot water beating down on my back. I didn't realize just how stressed I was until now, feeling all the knots coming loose in my muscles. This is exactly what I need too. Don't want to be too keyed up before the game tonight.

When I get back to the lockers, my phone is buzzing against the bench. I look at it, hoping it's either Brittney or Colter calling me back.

No luck. Just another one of those damn spam calls I'm getting real sick of. Whatever the fuck they're selling, I don't want it.

This time I'm just pissed off enough to answer.

"What?" I growl into the phone.

"Oh! You answered! We've been trying to reach you—"

"About my car's extended warranty? No, thanks."

I pull the phone away from my ear, ready to hit the *end call* button, then a few choice words catch my attention.

"—Vegas. There was a mistake and—"

I bring the phone back up to my ear. "Wait. What's going on? Start over."

The person sighs like they're exasperated by me. "My name is Debbie and I'm with the Heart Song Chapel here in Las Vegas. We've been trying to reach you for quite some time now about your marriage certificate."

"What about it?"

"Here in Vegas, you have ten business days to file your marriage certificate with the county registrar's office. If you fail to file your certificate, your marriage is not legal."

"Yes, but that was included in the package. You would file for us."

"Correct, sir. However, when they went to file your certificate, they noticed a discrepancy with the signature. Somebody signed as Daisy Duck."

There must be a mistake. I remember the ceremony. I remember reciting our vows, and I remember signing that document.

There's no way.

"Sir, are you still there?"

"I'm still here. What…what exactly does this all mean?"

"Your marriage…sir, you are not legally married."

We lost.

It's not the first time we've lost this season and it won't be the last, but tonight we lost for one reason and one reason only.

Me.

My head wasn't even kind of in the game. I couldn't concentrate for shit. I let the puck just skate by me, I took bad penalties, and I skated like I was playing peewee hockey all over again.

Tonight's loss is solely on my shoulders.

And it's all because I'm not married to my wife.

Well, not my wife, apparently.

I still can't believe it. How could they have let such a huge mistake slip right through their fingers like that? How could we not know? How could we not remember?

And more than that—why? Why did Ryan sign the certificate with a fake name? Does that mean she knew all along we were making a massive mistake? Does that mean even in her crazy drunken haze, she didn't want to be married to me? Does that mean if I confront her with this truth, she'll leave me?

I clutch my chest, rubbing at a spot just over my heart.

Coach comes charging into the room, hands on his hips. He's pissed and disappointed. His eyes land right on me, and he shakes his head with disgust.

That's okay. I'm disgusted with me too.

"Well, that was...something, and not something good, that's for damn sure. I expect that the next time we're out on that ice, we all have our heads in the game and we come out swinging. We got it?"

A round of affirmations goes around the room, but it's weak.

"I said, do we fucking got it?" Coach yells.

Everyone screams louder this time, me included, because I know that's what he's waiting for.

"Good. Now hit the showers and get out of here. I'm tired of looking at you." He sends me one last pointed glare, then stomps out of the room.

I begin stripping my gear off as Collin slides up next to me.

"Yo, man, what the fuck was that out there? You were playing like dog shit."

"Not now, Col. I'm not in the mood."

"Not in the mood? Not in the fucking mood? I don't give two shits if you're in the mood or not. You let this entire fucking team down and I want an explanation."

"What's that famous NHL quote? It's always we, never I?"

He does not appreciate my sarcasm one bit, his features falling into a mean scowl that could rival one of my own.

"I don't know what the fuck is up your ass, but whatever it is, you need to pull it out. It's not just you out on that ice, you know. It's not like you to be selfish like that."

I squeeze my eyes shut because he's right. It's not like me. "Having a bad night is all."

"What's going on? Talk to me."

"It's…" I shake my head. "It's Ryan."

His face fills with concern immediately. "Is she okay? What happened?"

"She's fine. She… I…" I toss myself down onto the bench, cradling my head in my hands.

Collin drops down beside me.

"Dude. What is going on? Did she finally realize you're ugly and leave you?"

I don't even have the energy to laugh.

"It's fake."

"It's fake?" He leans closer. "Your marriage?" he whispers. "Yeah, I know. It's been fake, man."

"No. It's *really* fake."

"What? What do you mean? I'm not following."

"She didn't sign it."

"Didn't sign what?"

"The certificate. She didn't sign the certificate."

His brows shoot up, finally beginning to understand. "That means…"

"We're not married. We were never married."

"Oh fuck."

Oh fuck indeed.

It's been three days since I found out about the marriage certificate, and I still haven't told Ryan.

How exactly do you tell your fake wife she isn't really your fake wife at all? And how do you tell her when what you really want is for her to be your real wife?

I take a deep breath, hands shaking as I push open the front door.

Tonight. I'll tell her tonight.

"Hey!" She beams at me. "I thought for sure you'd be at least another hour."

She's standing in the kitchen wearing one of my shirts and a pair of little sleep shorts. She's barefoot, and it's very obvious with the way her nipples are pressing against the shirt that she's not wearing a bra.

She looks fucking gorgeous, and I can't help when I cross the kitchen and sweep her into my arms, slanting my mouth over hers.

I kiss her hard. I kiss her deep.

I kiss her for all the times I'm not going to be able to kiss her anymore.

When I finally pull away, we're both gasping for air.

She peers up at me, her eyes glassy with lust. "Wow. What was that for?"

"Missed you."

"I missed you too. Is everything okay?"

"Yeah, everything is great."

"Are you sure?" She studies me closely. Too fucking closely.

"Actually, no. Everything isn't fine."

I turn her away from me, pressing her against the counter, grinding my hard cock against her ass. I gather her long hair into my fists, tugging on it not so lightly.

A small moan escapes her, her head lolling back, enjoying the bite of pain she's no doubt feeling.

"W-What's wrong?"

It's on the tip of my tongue to tell her the truth.

I should tell her the truth.

I *want* to tell her the truth.

I want to tell her I love her. Tell her I can't imagine a day of my life without her in it and I want this to be real more than anything I've ever wanted before.

But I don't say any of that.

Instead, I say, "You're wearing too many clothes."

Then, I lift her shirt and push her shorts down her legs. I strip her underwear from her body and bend her over the counter. I fist her hair and grab her hips and I fuck her hard.

Raw.

Rough.

I slide into her pussy over and over again as the sounds of her moans and our skin slapping together fill the quiet kitchen.

And I pretend she's mine just one last time.

CHAPTER 21

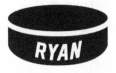

RYAN

Something is off with Rhodes.

I could tell when he came home. There was just something in his eyes that didn't seem right to me.

I don't know what it is either. He wouldn't talk after he fucked me against the kitchen counter. Instead, he took me back to the bedroom and did it all over again.

Something was going on. I could feel it.

But instead of forcing him to talk, I let him take what he needed, thinking maybe in the morning, things would be different.

I was wrong, because that was two days ago and nothing has changed. Something is off, and I want so badly to know what it is. I've already decided that tonight when he comes home from his game, I'm confronting him.

My phone buzzes against the desk with my reminder that I have about five minutes to finish prepping for my live video.

In an effort to grow my YouTube channel and get my

views up, I've been doing live makeup tutorials. At first, I was really nervous because it's awkward being in front of the camera on a good day, but being live in front of the camera? Downright terrifying. If I mess up, everybody is there to see it. If I say the wrong thing, everybody can hear it. It's a huge risk to take.

But sometimes you have to play the algorithm game, and right now, I'm playing it.

And it's working.

Thanks to all my newfound followers and views, I've been able to double my income over the last two months. If I keep this up, I'll be right on track to get my student loans paid off when our one-year agreement is up.

My chest pinches with discomfort.

I don't want to think about that. I don't want to think about how I'm going to have to walk away from the man I'm in love with.

My timer goes off with a thirty-second warning, and I sit down in my chair in front of my setup. I stretch my neck a few times to get rid of the tightness forming from my nerves. I check my teeth in the mirror, then paste on my brightest smile just as the feed goes live.

"Hey, you beauty babes!" I wave at the camera. "I'm so glad you're able to join me today. I can see we already have…oh wow, there are five hundred of you here. That's…oh! It just jumped. Wow. Twelve hundred already? Holy…oh my gosh, there are five thousand of you! This is crazy! This is the most viewers I've ever had at once. Thank you so much."

I smile at the camera, but behind the scenes, my heart is beating rapidly. I have never had this many people on my live videos before.

I glance down to make sure I actually put on clothes just to make sure I'm not naked and that's why everybody is running to watch the feed.

Nope, I'm definitely dressed.

The views climb. And climb. And climb. Before I know it, I'm sitting at 250,000 people watching.

I'm shocked. I'm overwhelmed.

"Wow," I say nervously to the camera. "This is… wow! Your girl is a little nervous over here, not going to lie." I chuckle, hoping it doesn't sound as fake as it feels. "Okay, let's just dive into it, huh? For today's look, I am going with something a little fun, a little funky. I was thinking about turning myself into Alice from *Alice in Wonderland*. What do you think? That sound good?"

My phone vibrates loudly against my desk, pulling my attention.

"Oh, sorry about that. Let me just turn that off really quick."

I pick it up and see Harper's name flashing across my screen. I hit ignore on the call, but before I can even set my phone down, texts start coming through.

Harper: CALL ME!!!

. . .

Harper: NOW!

Harper: Do not read the comments. Call me. Please.

I have literally never clicked on comments so fast in my life.

And I regret it immediately.

Hundreds upon hundreds spill onto the page. They're coming in so fast I can hardly keep up with them.

GirlyGirl18: Is it true?

BathAndBeautyWorks: My god. Shut up. No way.

User256468: You're not married???

BombBabe: Oh my god, what a psycho lying to us about being married.

MakeupMaddy: Liar, liar, liar.

. . .

Hockeyluvr2: OMG, I just feel so bad for Adrian Rhodes. Like, this chick has been using his name and lying like crazy about being married to him. Can you say crazy??? Poor Adrian!!

FckIt: Lying bitch.

BossyBabe3: What a slut.

User0585: Like seriously, how pathetic can you be?? Lying about being married to somebody like WTF?

Liar. Not married.

What the hell is going on?

"So, um, I don't really know what's happening here. It seems like I'm having some possible technical difficulties and…"

I fumble my way through the words, unable to take my eyes off the comments that are still coming in.

Kickrocks4: WHORE!!!!!

URLUVRGIRL: Can you say D-E-S-P-E-R-A-T-E much?!

. . .

User835088: hahahaha how sad

PrincessPeaches8: Yeah I am totally unsubbing now. LAME.

KensBarbieGurl: Totally disappointed

RhodesLuvr: Guess this means my man is officially back on the market then!

CometsFan96: GOOD RIDDANCE! Rhodes doesn't need distractions this season. BACK 2 BACK BABY!

TheBeastsBelle: Sad sad SAD! But at least Rhodes is free now!

I don't know what to do. I don't know what to say.

So, I switch my computer off. Disconnect everything.

My heart is hammering so hard in my chest that I feel dizzy and it's a struggle to drag air through my lungs.

I don't understand what's happening but the things they're saying… They send a bad feeling through my gut. I clutch my stomach, suddenly feeling nauseated.

My phone buzzes against the desk, scaring the shit out of me. I watch it buzz, seeing that it's Rhodes calling me. I have never wanted to both answer and ignore a call so badly in my life.

With shaky hands, I hit the green button and place the phone against my ear. "H-Hello?"

"Oh, thank fuck. Listen, whatever you do, do *not* go online, okay?"

"Well, it's a little late for that. I was literally just on a live video, and I started getting all these crazy comments."

"Oh shit."

"People were calling me a liar and a slut and saying all kinds of mean things, untrue things."

"Ryan…"

"They said we aren't married."

Silence.

Complete and utter silence.

"Rhodes?" I ask tentatively. "Is it true? Are we not married?"

He sighs. And just with that sigh, I know.

"No, Ryan, we aren't married."

After completely screwing up my life, I ended up in the same spot I was trying to avoid.

On Harper's couch.

Okay, fine, so maybe it's not on her couch. I'm in her spare bedroom, but it's still the same result.

A soft knock sounds on the door as it swings inward.

Poe stands, ready to protect me if need be, like the badass she is. I run my hand down her back, calming her.

Harper pokes her head around the frame. "Hey, good morning."

She says it like I'm a skittish little kitten about to run off.

"All right," I say, holding my hand up. "Before you walk any farther into this room, I need you to take the kid gloves off."

Harper makes a show of pretending to peel gloves off her hands, then rolls her sleeves up like she's ready to fight and continues into the room. She settles in on the end of the bed and stares at me.

The longer she stares, the deeper she frowns, and the deeper she frowns, the more annoyed I get.

I sigh. "Just say it. Whatever it is you're in here to say, just say it."

"I don't have anything to say. I just wanted to see if you were doing okay."

"I'm fine, Harper. Totally fine. There's nothing to worry about."

"Nothing to worry about? Ryan, your husband isn't your husband. You married a guy in Vegas, decided to stay fake married to him for a year, fell in love, and then found out the entire thing was a lie and you never got married in the first place. What do you mean there's nothing to worry about?"

Once she says it out loud like that, it sounds absolutely crazy. And, well, it is kind of crazy.

I haven't spoken with Rhodes in days. I know it was probably immature and completely unhelpful for me to run, but I needed space. Needed a fresh environment to clear my head. Every time I looked around his house, I felt like my lungs were going to give up.

I'm upset with him. Not because we're not married—because that somehow just feels like a technicality at this point. No, I'm upset with him because he *knew* we weren't married, and he hid it from me for days only for me to have to find out on social media during a damn live video.

It was mortifying.

And the worst part is, I don't know what this means for us.

I need to talk to him—desperately so—but I'm not ready.

I need more time. I need to process. I need to think. I need to figure out what the hell it is we are going to do.

I feel like I'm in Las Vegas all over again, stressing about what I'm going to do with my life. Only this time, I don't feel hopeful about my future. I just feel really, really sad.

And scared. I'm worried about my career that I've worked so hard for blowing up in my face. I'm worried about paying for my grandmother's care.

I'm worried about how I'm going to forgive the man I love for hiding such a big thing from me.

"If it's any consolation," Harper says, "Collin says he looks like shit."

I laugh. "To be fair, Collin always says Rhodes looks like shit."

"True," Harper agrees. "Have you talked with him?"

"Not yet. But I will."

"Good." She nods. "That's good. I, uh, might have pulled a total you and done some social media digging."

"You did?"

"Yep, and I found the name and personal email of the person who published the article about your marriage not being real."

"And?"

"And I politely but firmly asked her who the hell tipped her off on this."

"And?" I prompt again.

"You were right. That Brittney is a bitch."

I fucking knew it.

Something deep in my gut knew things were off when she accosted me at the gallery. There was something so strange about the way she was phrasing things oddly, questioning my wedding ring, and stalking my social media account so closely. It made me super uncomfortable. I know Rhodes tried to talk with her and figure out what was going on, but he couldn't get ahold of her. Now I know why. She was spending all her free time trying to figure out whether or not Rhodes and I are actually married and then plotting her revenge.

"I don't get it. She's the one who dumped him. Why would she care that he got married or if his marriage is legit or not? She clearly didn't care about him when she told him to take a hike."

"Um, because bitches be crazy. That's why." Harper says it like it's the most obvious answer in the world.

"Yes, they do be crazy, but…" I shake my head. "You should have heard the way she was talking about him when she saw the photo of him at the gallery. She was so…*mean.* Just plain cruel."

"Maybe she was jealous?"

"Of what? Me?"

"Uh, yeah, you're kind of a catch, Ryan."

I wave my hand down my body. "Ah, yes, such a catch." I admit it, it's probably been three days since I've last showered. I've been wearing the same pair of sweats for at least two of them, and I don't remember the last time I changed my shirt. My hair is a greasy, tangled mess and my makeup is from several days ago.

Simply put: I look like shit.

"Okay, well, maybe not like *now* now, but generally, you are a catch."

I laugh. Leave it to Harper to make me feel better when I'm feeling my worst.

She winks at me, then the mood in the room switches back to that somberness that seems to be holding steady.

"What are you going to do?"

I lift my shoulders. "I don't know."

"You love him, right?"

"So, so much. He's…everything I didn't know I wanted. He's so much more than meets the eye. I love him more than I could have ever imagined. But, Harper, what if he doesn't love me back? I mean, this whole thing was a sham, a big ruse so he didn't get in trouble with his team. None of it is real. Hell, he had to be drunk to get married to me in the first place. Before that, we barely even spoke to each other. He mildly tolerated me on the best of days. I…I don't know what I'm going to do if he doesn't love me back."

The frown that seems to be permanently etched into her face deepens. She reaches over, placing her hand on mine. "If he doesn't love you back, he's a fool, and I watch a lot of horror movies. I have some great ideas on how to get away with murder and destroy bodies and evidence like *this*." She snaps her fingers for emphasis.

I laugh. "That's not terrifying at all. Remind me not to piss you off."

"I'm just saying." She shrugs. "But seriously, Ryan, if Rhodes is too dumb to see that you're the best thing that's ever happened to him, he doesn't deserve you. If you ask me, though, I don't think him not loving you is something you're going to have to worry about. I see the way he looks at you, and it's the same way Collin looks at me. I think maybe you just need to talk to him and be honest with him about what you want. Because maybe you want the same things."

"What if we don't want the same things?"

"Then we start digging."

CHAPTER 22

RHODES

Everybody in the locker room is looking at me like I'm about to break, and it's really starting to piss me off.

I've been keeping my head down and trying to avoid confrontation all week. Luckily, Collin, Miller, and Lowell have all stepped in to help keep everything a little less crazy.

But it's hard when your teammates are looking at you like they can't trust you. It's hard for me because, on one hand, I meant to lie, but on the other, I didn't.

It's all so confusing.

Coach has been livid with me all week, and my ice time reflects that. I've barely been getting five minutes since everything went to shit.

My mom is pissed at me. My teammates are pissed at me. The organization is pissed at me. And worst of all, Ryan is pissed at me.

I miss her. I miss her so fucking much it hurts. I didn't know I could hurt like this. I thought I knew pain when my life changed forever when the skate blade connected with my face, but I was wrong.

It's nothing compared to this.

I want to talk to her more than anything, but I also want to give her space.

I fully understand why she's upset with me. I wasn't upfront about knowing the marriage certificate never got submitted. I slept on the knowledge of that for days, knowing it changed everything.

And I did it because I was scared. Absolutely fucked out of my head. Worried I was going to lose her.

In the end, I might have lost her anyway.

"All right, everybody. Suit up. Hit the ice for warmups. I want you to go out there and play hard. Hit hard. Win battles in the corners. And make sure Florida knows this is *our* house. We got it?" The room cheers. "Good. Now get out there and win a fucking hockey game."

Everyone is buzzing, that pregame high coursing through our veins.

They're ready for this.

I'm ready for this.

I'm especially ready for this because Colter plays for Florida now, and I fully plan to land every hit on him possible tonight.

Denver did some digging for me and found out that the informant for the article who blew this whole mess up was none other than Brittney. I guess she's been digging into our marriage from the beginning. When she came up blank on finding evidence, she concluded it was fake and tipped off the press, who then did the work they're so good at.

It's funny. I don't think she even knew I was aware of the certificate mishap. I think she was trying to get one over on me and shock me.

I don't care about her trying to hurt me. I just care about Ryan hurting.

So tonight, we're playing by hockey rules, and Colter is going to pay.

Warmups are uneventful. Colter stays to his side and I stay over to mine, but I make sure to stare him down the entire time, letting him know his time is coming.

By the time he's skating off the ice, he looks like he's about to piss his pants.

Collin comes up and claps me on the back as we head down the tunnel for puck drop. "Good, man?"

"Yep. Fucking dandy."

A grin pulls up one side of his lips. "You're totally going to fuck him up, aren't you?"

"Yep."

He laughs, and I have a feeling he might get his licks in too.

The game kicks off, and within five minutes, the teams are already coming to fisticuffs courtesy of our captain running Colter into the boards.

It was a clean hit, a solid hit. But Florida didn't like it.

After that, we score, making it 1–0. Luckily for Colter, we've yet to share a shift out on the ice. No doubt something carefully orchestrated by Coach. During the second period, he gets lucky again, and so do we. We're up 3–0.

And then, finally, in the third period, when we are stomping their asses 5–0, his time comes.

We step out on the ice together, and I immediately drop the gloves. No preamble, just straight for the guy. He knew it was coming, so he was prepared.

"I'm not looking for a fight tonight, Rhodes," he tries to reason.

"That's too fucking bad. You gotta answer for what you did."

"What I did? I didn't do shit! That was all Brittney!"

I grab his sweater, finally getting the fucker to hold still, and we trade blows.

Over and over and over again.

"Stop, stop!" he screams. "Fuck, man! I didn't do anything!"

"No, but your fucking fiancée did."

"We're not even engaged, asshole."

"What?" I loosen my grip on him and he goes tumbling to the ice on his ass. The refs hold me back as if I'm about to hop on top of him. "What did you say?"

"We're not even engaged. It was all for show."

For show? She was never even engaged.

What the fuck?

"She was mad at you because you wouldn't propose to her. So, she made up this big elaborate thing, hoping you'd get jealous and break up the engagement. But no, you had to go get fucking married to some other little slut."

And that's when I truly see red.

This has to be the worst week of my life, and that includes the week I got my scar.

Ryan and I aren't married.

I'm in love with her and she won't talk to me.

And now I'm fucking suspended for fighting.

Okay, so maybe not for fighting. It was more like slaughtering.

I lost it after he called Ryan a slut. Completely lost all sense of being and just wailed on him. I don't remember anything that happened after that. All I could focus on was beating him to a bloody pulp. And watching the videos back, that's exactly what I did.

I don't feel bad about it either. If that makes me wrong, then I don't care.

"Totally fucked this one up," my agent says as he slides onto the stool next to me.

I've had my ass planted on this stool at Slapshots for two hours now. My sentence was handed down earlier this afternoon, and I can't seem to make myself go home because it makes me too damn sad. All I do is think about Ryan and hockey and everything I'm missing out on.

"Think it's safe to say I am totally boned."

"Six games, Rhodes. And for *that.* It looks like petty retaliation." He holds out two fingers to the bartender, then nods toward my beer. "Doesn't look good."

"I know."

The bartender slides two beers in front of us. One for me and one for him.

"Other than this little blemish on your hockey career, how are you feeling?"

"Like shit. Utter shit."

Shep laughs at me. "Yep, been there."

I've never meant those words more in my life mostly because I can't remember a time when I've felt like this. After my accident, I felt awful. But this? This is a whole new level of awful.

It's excruciating. Body-aching painful.

And I have nobody to blame but myself.

I know I shouldn't have kept the truth about our marriage from Ryan. It was stupid. Easily the dumbest thing I could have done after we worked so hard to build a genuine relationship and respect for one another.

But…I was scared.

God. That sounds so fucking ridiculous, but it's true.

I was scared that if she didn't have a reason to be married to me, she wouldn't stay.

And why should she? I'm grumpy as shit half the time and I'm not the best at expressing my emotions. Nobody wants to deal with that shit, especially not someone like Ryan.

Someone so smart and funny and gorgeous and way fucking out of my league.

She doesn't have a reason to stay—I know it and she does too.

I just…I hope that she does.

I miss her. I miss her laugh, her smile. I miss the way she looks first thing in the morning and the way she smells. I miss her so damn much that I hid her pillow from my housekeeper, so she didn't wash away Ryan's scent.

I'm a sick, sick man.

Sick and sad and so stupid.

"Why does love hurt like this?"

"No fucking clue, man, but it blows." He runs a hand through his hair. "I'm sorry Denver couldn't get out in front of this one. Totally blindsided us all."

I laugh, but there's no humor to it. "You can say that again."

I pick up my fourth beer of the hour and knock the rest of it back in one drink. I reach for the one Shep just bought me and sip at that too.

"Do you really think drinking away your troubles is the best thing to do given your history?"

I glare over at him. "Mind your business, Shep."

He lifts his hands up. "Just saying, last time that did not turn out so well for you."

He's got that right.

"Have you talked to her?"

I shake my head. "Not yet."

"Do you know what you're going to say to her when you do?"

"Not a fucking clue."

"Well, in my experience, it helps if you tell her you're in love with her. Girls are really into the whole 'being emotionally available' thing."

I laugh at that. "Is that what's wrong with me? Am I just not emotionally available enough?"

"Honestly? I think you're a little too emotionally available."

Well, that's a first.

"Listen, I'm going to say this in the nicest way possible, but…that scar really fucked you up in more ways than one. Yeah, it made that ugly mug of yours even uglier. But it messed you up where it really counts." He taps the side of his head with his forefinger. "You're stuck up here, man. Like totally stuck up here. You are just a giant closed-off mess because you're so damn worried about what everybody sees when they look at you that you forget about all the other important parts. Not to be a walking fucking cliché or anything, but it's what's on the inside that counts the most. And your insides are a little screwy."

He's right. I know he's right. I am messed up in the head from my scar. Messed up in the head because it's what everyone sees first. And sometimes, it's all people see. After a while, it gets really hard to crack the code of who is who.

"Can I ask you a question?" Shep says.

"Not like I have anything better to do right now. Go for it."

"How come you married her?"

"I don't know, I was drunk."

He gives me a look that says I'm full of shit. "Try again."

"Man, I don't fucking know. I was drunk. I was like out-of-my-mind drunk."

"There's nothing in your mind that sticks out as to why? A reason for it being her? Out of all the people you could have done this with, you did it with her?"

I lift my shoulders. "I…well, I guess she felt safe."

"Safe?"

"Yeah. Safe. I felt like I could be myself around her and I never had to put on any sort of front or put up any walls."

"And why is that? Why did you feel like that with her?"

"My eyes."

"Your eyes?"

"Yeah. She always looked me in my eyes. A lot of people don't look me in the eye. They just look at my scar, and then they're afraid to meet my eyes because they don't like what they see or they don't want me to see how they really feel, but Ryan? She always looked me in my eyes, even when I didn't want her to, and I thought that was brave. I thought *she* was brave, and that made me want to be brave. Kind of stupid because, I mean, look at me. I'm a giant, scary, beastly dude getting showed up by this little beauty who is bolder than I could ever dream to be."

"So be it."

"Huh?"

"Be it. Be brave. Be brave for her. Be brave for yourself. Tell her how you feel. Tell her what you want. And tell her so damn loudly she has no choice but to listen to you. Just be brave."

CHAPTER 23

RYAN

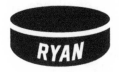

"She's cheatin'!"

"Cheatin'? You can't cheat at word searches!" Grams hollers back at Harper.

"Oh, bullshit, you old coot. You're cheating and you know it."

"Show me how to cheat, then, Ms. Know-It-All."

I grin at the two of them as they bicker back and forth.

We've been sitting at Grams' apartment for the last two hours doing word searches. Harper got the brilliant idea to set a timer an hour ago and see who can beat the word search the fastest. Grams has beat her every time.

"I don't know how, but I'm going to figure it out."

Never mind that my grandmother does about twenty-five of these a day. She's practically an expert at them by now. There's no way Harper is going to beat her, but apparently, she's going to keep trying. She sets the clock, then calls out a countdown, and they're off to the races all over again.

I've been sitting here trying not to look at my phone to check and see how many times Rhodes has not called me.

It's been two weeks of silence, two weeks of absolute heartache.

I wanted so badly to reach out to him after I saw his fight and again when I saw he was handed a six-game suspension because of it, but I didn't know what to say.

Still don't know what to say.

Grams wasn't happy with me when she found out my marriage wasn't real…for all of like two seconds. Then her romance-loving heart was over the moon that I fell in love with him. She said it was that "movie-worthy" kind of moment and if I didn't fix it, she'd never forgive me.

I want to fix it, but what do you say to your fake husband that you fell in love with?

It's weird because on one hand, I understand why Rhodes kept it from me. It was easier that way. Legally married or not, we'd already told everyone. We kind of didn't have a choice but to go through with it unless we wanted to come clean about everything, and I think that would have caused even more of a headache.

But for Rhodes to keep it from me the way he did? That hurt. I thought we built trust with one another. Thought we respected each other. I thought that what we had was real, even if it started for not-so-real reasons. And I naively thought he felt about me how I feel about him.

You don't let the person you love be blindsided like

that though.

"Game's on!" Grams' roommate, Nancy, calls from the other room, drawing everyone's attention. "We got hockey butts on TV, ladies!"

I'd be lying if I said the urge to walk into that living room and watch it isn't eating a hole in me right now. Tonight is Rhodes' first game back since his suspension, and I am dying to see him play.

I didn't realize how in love I fell with the sport. Not having hockey in my life over the last few weeks has been weird. I miss it. I miss the thrill of watching the guys fly down the ice. I miss the crashing into the boards. I miss the crazy shots thrown at the net that should never go in but somehow always do. I miss the announcers being total goofballs and mispronouncing so many names.

I miss hockey, and most of all, I miss my hockey player.

I try to ignore the pit in my stomach that's been steadily growing the last few weeks.

"Well, I don't know about you ladies, but I'm going to go watch some hockey," Grams says, rising from her spot at the kitchen table.

Harper's wide eyes find mine to see what the hell I'm going to do.

I know she's dying to watch, but she's trying to be a supportive friend. That's why she's here today instead of at the game cheering her fiancé on. Solidarity and all that.

She lifts a brow, and I can see the excitement in her

eyes. "What do you say? You want to go watch some grown men be paid entirely too much money to chase around a vulcanized rubber disc on frozen water with knife blades on their feet?"

Well, I guess that's one way to ask if I want to watch hockey.

"What the hell? I can't avoid the game forever."

"That's my girl!" Grams says.

We make our way into the living room just as the puck drops.

And there he is.

God, even looking at him on this awful, outdated television, he's beautiful. He looks different and the same all at once.

My heart aches just seeing him. My body yearns for him.

Harper and Grams take the two open spots on the couch, and I stand at the back, eyes glued to the television.

I don't look away for a single second, which means I don't miss the goal he scores just four minutes into the game. I don't miss the way the crowd erupts, screaming his name.

"BEEEAAASSSTTT!" they belt out.

And he smiles.

Adrian Rhodes *smiles.*

Full-blown, teeth-showing, cheek-splitting smile.

And it's breathtaking.

He's breathtaking.

Gameplay resumes, but not before everybody on the bench goes wild and congratulates him on the goal. They're clearly happy to have him back.

The Comets score another goal in the first period, but unfortunately, Vancouver comes back to score twice in the second to tie it up. At the beginning of the third, Rhodes takes a hit, and he goes down hard.

My breath catches in my throat, and I swear I don't breathe the entire time he's down on the ice. Collin and Lowell help him off and down the tunnel. I breathe a sigh of relief when the announcers tell us he's back on the bench and feeling fine.

It makes me both sad and happy I'm not currently there in the crowd.

With just three minutes to go, it's the damn rookie back to save the day, and the Comets take the win. Harper, Grams, Nancy, and I all cheer, glad the guys were able to make the comeback and win.

The postgame show starts, and I head to the kitchen to start on the dishes in Grams' sink. There's nothing on there for me to watch.

I'm about halfway into a sink full of dishes when I hear it.

Rhodes.

I whirl around, hands still soaking wet from the water, not caring that I'm dripping it everywhere.

"Adrian, can you tell us how it felt to be back out on the ice after missing six games?"

"Good."

I laugh at his one-syllable answer. Typical Rhodes.

"Adrian, can you walk us through that game where you got suspended? What happened?"

I lean closer to the TV, dying to know the details too.

He sits forward, lips nearly touching the microphone. He tugs the hat he's wearing down lower.

"What happened is that Joshua Colter said some very…" He runs a hand over his jaw, trying to find the right words. "Uh, *unsportsmanlike* things about a person who is very special to me. And, well, I wasn't going to let that happen."

He sits back again, crossing his arms over his chest.

"There seems to be a lot of bad blood between you and Mr. Colter. Is this because he's engaged to your ex-girlfriend?" someone else asks.

"Uh, no. It's because he's a dick."

Several people in the room snicker, a few gasp.

Me? I cackle.

"Adrian, can you tell us what's going on with your marriage to beauty influencer Ryan Bell? It was announced over the summer that you two had tied the knot during a weekend in Las Vegas, but now there are reports that the marriage never happened. Can you elaborate on that for us?"

He shifts around in his chair, clearly uncomfortable being in front of all the cameras and being put on the spot.

"Come on, let's stick to hockey, huh?" Someone speaks up for him, and it sounds like Collin offscreen.

"Look, I'm only going to talk about this one time, so everybody go ahead and get your little tape recorders ready." He pauses, waiting for them to do just that. "You all good?"

There's a murmuring amongst the crowd, confirming they are ready to go.

Rhodes spins his ballcap backward, and I know the move is significant. He's putting his scar on display.

My chest swells with pride.

He sits forward, lips to the microphone, and I hold my breath for the second time tonight.

"The announcement made this summer was the result of a drunken night in Las Vegas where Ryan Bell and I were led to believe we had gotten married. Honestly, it was a silly mistake that came courtesy of my good friend Jose and his buddy Jack, and a little thing called poor decision-making." A few people laugh. "Truthfully, we had no business doing what we did, and I regret it."

My heart sinks.

"But I don't regret it for the reasons most people might think." He takes a deep breath, then exhales slowly. "I regret it because I didn't do it for the right reasons. I did it because my heart hurt, and I wanted it to stop hurting. That is the *only* reason I regret it. I don't regret who I married, and I don't regret the last few months I've spent falling in love with my wife. And yes, I said wife. Because to me, for all intents and purposes, we did get married. The only thing we didn't do was sign the certificate. But we took vows. We exchanged rings. And we made promises that, if Ryan forgives me for this whole mess, I intend to keep."

The room is silent.

Completely still.

Then, it erupts.

Everyone is talking over one another, and it's nearly impossible to decipher what's being asked. I hear my name. I hear Rhodes' name. I hear words like annulment and divorce and deceit.

Rhodes just leans down into the microphone and says, "No further questions. Thank you."

Then he disappears off stage.

And I'm left standing here stunned.

"Ryan?" Harper asks quietly, moving to stand in front of me. "Are you...okay?"

"I...don't know," I answer honestly.

"That"—Grams points to the TV—"is what us romance lovers call a grand gesture. This is the part in the movie where you run through the airport for him and confess *your* love before he hops a flight to Paris, never to be seen again." She grabs my shoulders. "How do you feel, Ryan?"

How do I feel?

How do I *feel*?

I feel...shocked. Stunned.

And so damn in love with him it hurts.

I'm mad and hurt and confused, but this is it—an ugly moment.

I can't give up now just because it's hard. I can't walk away just because my heart is hurting. If I think Rhodes is truly worth it—and I do—I need to fight for what I want.

Because these ugly moments? They make all the pretty ones even more beautiful.

"I love him," I say.

Grams grins, squeezing my shoulders. "Then go. Go find your airport. Go confess how you feel."

"But what—"

"I swear if you say some silly shit like 'But what if he doesn't love me,' I will knock you upside the head," Nancy says. "If you don't get your ass out that door and find your man in the next ten seconds, I'm taking off after him myself."

I look to Harper, and she nods, shoving her car keys at me. "Go. I'll text Collin to see where he's at."

She doesn't have to tell me twice.

I hop in the car and drive.

Truthfully, I don't need Harper or Collin to tell me where he's at because I know Rhodes.

I *know* him.

It's crazy to think that just a few months ago, he was just the teammate of my best friend's boyfriend.

Now? Now he's my world. That Prince Charming I've been waiting for.

He's my Beast, and I'm his Beauty.

We make no sense together, but I'll be damned if I let that stop us.

A message chimes over the infotainment center of Harper's new car and I press the *Read* button.

Harper: He's at Slapshots.

I knew it.

With it being a game night, I'm not expecting to find parking, but somehow luck is on my side, and I maneuver the car into a spot just across the street.

I waste no time darting across the intersection, ignoring the beeps and shouts from drivers, and yank open the door to the beloved bar.

The place is packed, but it doesn't stop me from spotting Rhodes instantly. He's so huge, he's kind of hard to miss.

God. Just seeing him sitting across the bar… My fingers itch to touch him. My body longs to be near him. I want so damn badly to throw myself in his lap and press my lips to his.

On shaky legs, I cross the bar and slide up next to him.

I feel the air crackle between us almost instantly.

I signal for the bartender and place an order. When he returns with four shots, I slide two to Rhodes and keep the others to myself.

Then, with a steadying breath, I turn to my husband.

"Want to hear a love story?"

CHAPTER 24

RHODES

A warm body slides onto the stool next to me, signaling to the bartender for a drink. "I'll take two shots each of Jose and Jack."

"Coming right up," the bartender says, turning to pour the shots.

He's only gone a minute or two, then he's placing the shots in front of the person next to me.

They slide a shot of each my way.

"Want to hear a love story?"

"I'm not really one for romance, but I'll bite."

She rests her elbow on the bar top, taking a shot glass in her hand. "I met this guy last year. He was the best friend of my best friend's boyfriend. If that's not confusing, I don't know what is. Anyway, I guess we became…allies of sorts. We weren't really friends, but we weren't *not* friends either. We were shoved into the same group activities whenever anyone could coax him out of his big, dark castle. Oh, he has a castle, by the way. How cool is that?"

"I think a big, dark castle sounds nice."

"Hmm. Maybe you should meet my friend, then. You'd probably get along." She waves her hand. "So anyway, this past summer, we all took a vacation to Las Vegas. A little fun, a little gambling, and some drinking. Lots and lots of drinking. Too much of it for certain. Then, like a total Prince Charming swooping in to save the day, guess who offers to take care of me?"

"Oh wait, don't tell me—it's the best friend of the best friend's boyfriend?"

"Yes!" She slaps the bar top. "What are the freakin' odds?"

"I'd say pretty good considering he was forced to take care of you. He did not choose it."

She narrows her eyes. "Anyway. He's doing the prince thing, taking care of me, making sure I don't choke on my own vomit. You know, the usual."

"He sounds like a really good dude."

"He was. But in a crazy twist of events, it was suddenly me, the princess, taking care of the prince. You see, he had his heart broken, and he needed it mended. So being the selfless soul I am, I stepped up."

"How kind of you."

"Right? I took him out dancing and drinking and gave him a magical night he'll never forget."

"Oh, no. You gave him herpes, didn't you?"

The look she gives me is murderous. "No. Better. I gave him a ring. Or he gave me a ring. I really can't remember because I was shit-faced."

"Wait. I thought you were taking care of the prince?"

"At that point, we were taking care of each other."

"Okay, okay. So, what happens next?"

"Well, in the wee hours of the not-so-morning, we wake up to find ourselves suddenly hitched and the evidence sprinkled all over social media."

"That sounds terrible."

"It was." She shudders. "See, the prince was this famous sports dude."

"Famous sports dude?"

"Yep. He literally played with his stick for a living."

I try not to choke on my beer.

"So, we did what any smart, quick-thinking pair would do—we faked it. We're talking move in together, pretend to be in love, fake it."

"And it worked? This ruse of yours?"

"Oh, certainly. Nobody was the wiser."

"Definitely not a single soul. You two sound like incredible actors."

"The best there ever was."

"What happened next?"

"Well, the dark moment."

"Dark moment?"

"Yeah." She nods. "You know, the big sad scene where everyone gets their heart broken and nothing feels like it's ever going to be right again."

"Ah. Yes. I am familiar with that."

"Well, it hit them *hard*."

"This is starting to sound less and less like a love story."

"That's because I'm not finished and you keep interrupting me, Rhodes."

I tuck my lips together, gesturing for her to continue.

She tosses her hair over her shoulder. "Anyway, then…ugh. No, no, never mind. You totally ruined it with all your talking!" She turns to me, daggers in her eyes.

"*I* ruined it with all *my* talking?"

"Yes! I was doing this super cute fairy-tale-story thing because I love fairy tales and then at the end I was going to be all *I love you, Adrian Rhodes* and you were going to be all"—she puffs her chest out, dropping her voice low—"*I love you too, baby.* And then we were going to make out like fools in public and live happily ever after."

"Okay, one, I do *not* sound like that."

"Oh, you totally do. All deep and growly. It's like—"

I kiss her.

I kiss her to shut her up and I kiss her because I can't stand not kissing her for another second.

It's a slow, languid kiss. Soft, gentle, and hopefully full of all the things I want to say to her.

She smiles against me when I pull away.

"Two," I continue, "I'm going to need to hear you say it again."

"All deep and growly like—"

"No. The *other* part."

"Oh, the part where I say I love you?" I nod, and she

brushes her lips against mine. "I love you, Adrian Rhodes."

"Yeah?"

She nods. "So much."

I sigh, feeling whole for the first time in a long time. "Good. Because I love you too."

"Yeah?"

"So much."

I kiss her again.

And again.

And again.

In fact, I don't stop kissing her until she's literally in my lap and we're making a scene.

"We should stop."

"We should."

But we don't.

Not until the owner of the bar comes over and taps us on the shoulder do we finally pull apart.

Ryan slips back onto her stool, and I dutifully stay on mine.

"I'm sorry," I tell her, keeping my hand on her leg.

Those lips that I can't seem to get enough of pull into a frown. "I know."

"I'm an idiot."

"I know that too."

I laugh. "God, I missed your smart mouth."

"I know *that* too." She winks, then sobers up quickly. "I won't lie, I'm still upset with you. It hurt to find out like I did. I wish you could have been honest with me. I thought…" She exhales shakily. "I thought we meant more than that to each other. I thought I deserved your honesty."

"We did. You did. You *do*. It was a stupid decision on my part, one made by a scared, foolish man."

"Scared?"

I gulp back the lump in my throat. "Of losing you. Of you realizing that you could do so much better than me."

She shakes her head. "When are you going to understand that you're enough, Rhodes?"

She takes my face in her hands, her thumb skating over my scar. I lean into her touch, needing it because it's been far too fucking long.

"You are enough," she says, "and I love you just the way you are."

I swallow, nodding. "I believe you."

She presses her lips to mine once more but this time it's softer. Slower. And I taste the truth of her words in her kiss.

When she pulls back, she says, "Did you mean what you said? During the postgame junket?"

"Which part? I said a lot. Mostly blocked it out."

"About keeping promises."

"Every fucking word."

"Good." She grins, lifting her shot glass. "To mistakes."

I lift mine too. "And promises."

We toss the shots back, and I wipe my hand across my mouth.

"So, you never did tell me how that story ended."

"Oh, that?" She grins. "It looks like it's still being written, but I'm predicting a happily ever after."

"I'm predicting you're right…*wife.*"

EPILOGUE

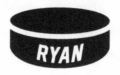

RYAN

"That woman is exhausting." I flop down into my chair and reach for my champagne glass, gulping back half of it in one go. "Remind me to never get married."

"Again." He tugs my hand into his lap, rubbing his fingertips over the gold band that still sits around my finger. He tried replacing it once with a big diamond set, but I refused. I love it too much. "Unless you want to. Have the big celebration and all that, I mean."

One weekend when the Comets were facing Vegas, Rhodes and I snuck off after the game and made our marriage official.

This time, we didn't share our elopement with the world. Just with Harper and Collin, the way it should have been from the beginning.

Surprisingly, Grams and Rhodes' parents were fine with it. I think they were all just happy we found a way to fall in love after the whole lying-to-the-world-and-it-blowing-up-in-our-faces fiasco.

Every now and then, Rhodes will ask if I want to do it the "right way," but I always give him the same answer.

"I already have everything I want." I trace the rose he has tattooed on his ring finger. He surprised me with it after the Comets ended their season early, losing in the second round of the playoffs. He said even though they lost, this way he'd always remember everything good that happened that season.

His lips twitch, fighting a smile. "Everything?"

"Well, I mean, I would like to get out of here, maybe have an orgasm or two. But beyond that, yes, everything."

He leans into me, his lips brushing against mine. "I think I could make that happen." He captures my mouth in a kiss, his tongue quickly pushing past my lips, ramping up the heat.

I'm lost in the moment, completely captivated by the way he commands my mouth, his tongue sliding over mine as his hand slides up my face and into my long blonde curls, pulling me closer.

I have no idea how much time passes before I hear a throat clearing.

"Excuse me, *Ryan*." Harper's mother practically hisses my name. I'm not sure if it's because she's never been a big fan of me or because I'm currently making out with my husband in the middle of her daughter's wedding. "I could really use your help with the—"

"Caterer? We have it covered, Mom." Harper places her hand on her mother's shoulder, pulling her attention.

"Why don't you go dance with Uncle Randy? I'm sure Aunt Blythe would love for you to take him off her hands for a bit. She looks tired."

Her mother glances over at the fun, older couple swinging around the dance floor. They both look like they're having a complete blast, but I know what Harper is trying to do—save me.

"Oh, all right then," her mother says. "Randy always was a handful."

Harper's mother sends me one last disapproving look before scurrying away.

"God, that woman is exhausting." Harper shakes her head, grabbing Rhodes' glass of champagne and downing it all at once.

"That's exactly what I said!"

"It's no wonder my sister moved here after her divorce. I mean, can you imagine having to deal with a cheating ex-husband *and* my mother?" Harper shudders, her lacy gray dress shaking around her. When she first suggested a gray dress, I thought she was out of her mind, but the beautiful ball gown-style garment fits her perfectly. "Speaking of my sister, have you seen her around here?"

"Actually, I think I saw her and Lowell step outside for a moment," Rhodes answers. "They seem to be getting along, which I suppose is good considering..."

He trails off, but we all know what he's alluding to. Hollis and Lowell meeting did not go as everyone had planned.

"Well, I'm glad. I was worried." Harper waves her hand. "Anyway, you two get back to Frenching. I'm going to find my husband." She giggles, bouncing on the heels of her black glitter Converse. "*Husband*—oh my gosh, I have one of those!" She claps her hands and takes off in pursuit of him.

I peer around the decorated venue and still can't believe it myself. With the black curtains and tablecloths, spooky décor, and low lighting, these two managed to have a beautiful dark-themed wedding in the middle of June and pull it off spectacularly.

I wave at Grams, who is currently rocking back and forth with Miller, her date for the evening. How she's managed to wrap the entire team around her finger in the last year, I have no clue, but it's adorable to see the grown men fussing over her. They're always rotating in and out of her apartment, helping to hang or move something, or just there to visit. I think most of them just miss their own grandparents, and since Grams is more than willing to have the company, they take as much advantage of it as she does.

She shoots me a wink and a thumbs-up. I shake my head, grinning.

My eyes drift over to Harper and Collin, who are now wrapped around each other in the middle of the dance floor. They look like picturesque newlyweds, heads bent together, smiles plastered on their faces. It's hard to believe there was ever a time when Harper was so reluctant to love Collin.

"I can't believe they're married."

"I can't believe *we're* married," Rhodes says. "It feels like just yesterday we were waking up hungover in Vegas, the sins of the night before hanging over us."

Some days it does feel like just yesterday.

Some days it feels like a lifetime ago.

But every day with Rhodes…every day feels just right.

Unable to stop myself, I lean over and press my lips to his.

He grins against my mouth. "What was that for, cupcake?"

"Cupcake?"

He shrugs. "Trying it out. Not a fan?"

"No. Not a fan, buttercup." His face pulls into the scowl I'm all too familiar with, and I laugh. "Not a fan?"

"Not even a little."

A quick shutter noise catches our attention.

"Sorry. Couldn't resist." The photographer grins at me. "Thanks again for recommending me for this job, Ryan. Photographing a Carolina Comets player's wedding…" He shakes his head in disbelief. "This is going to be such a bright spot in my portfolio."

"I'm glad you could fit them into your schedule, Winston. Who knows, with the way this team seems to be pairing off, you might have more projects in your future."

"Grams and Miller *do* seem pretty cozy," Rhodes remarks.

Winston laughs. "Speaking of cozy, I really don't

want to miss this moment." He takes off to grab a few shots as Miller drops Grams down into a dip, her mouth falling open in shock.

"That kid is way too smooth for his own good." Rhodes shakes his head then rises from his chair and holds his hand out to me. "All right, let's go show them up."

"*You* want to dance?"

"What? I dance."

I lift a brow. "Since when?"

He leans down, lips against my ear. "Don't pretend you don't remember our evening in Vegas. I distinctly remember someone asking to be spanked as we danced." My cheeks flame red, and he chuckles darkly. "That's what I thought."

He straightens and extends his palm once more with a cocky grin pulling at his lips. I place my hand in his, letting him pull me to my feet.

We make our way out onto the floor, and Rhodes spins me into his arms, tugging me close. My body lines up against his like we were made to do this together, pressing against one another in all the right places.

The song that's playing isn't even slow, but we don't care, swaying leisurely anyway.

"Can I ask you something?" he asks quietly.

"Of course."

"Do you remember why we decided to get married? The first time," he amends.

I shake my head. "No. That night is still fuzzy."

He nods. "For me too. I can remember feeling safe with you, feeling comfortable. And happy—though that could have been the alcohol." I laugh. "But I can't remember the moment we said fuck it and did it."

"I can't either. Sometimes I wish I could, but other times…I don't know. I kind of like the magic of it. They say you tell the truth when you're drunk, and maybe our truth was this."

"I had a crush on you, you know."

I pull my head back, looking up at him. "What? You did not."

"I did. That first time I saw you, under the arena lights, I thought you were gorgeous, and I had a crush on you. I mean, I didn't realize it then, but I do now. I think a big reason I was always extra grumpy to you was because you intimidated me."

"*I* intimidated *you*? I'm sorry, but have you *seen* your scowl?"

He laughs. "I'm being serious."

"I am too! You're scary when you're all…growly."

"Growly?"

"Yeah. You know…*beastly*."

"I've always hated that nickname."

"I can imagine why."

"But I don't hate it anymore."

"No? What changed?"

"I found my beauty."

I grin. "That was cheesy. Like romantic comedy cheesy."

"You loved it."

"I love *you*."

He captures my lips in a searing kiss, so quick and hot that I'm lucky he's holding me up right now because my knees can't take it.

"Do you think anyone will notice if we sneak away?"

"I sure as hell hope not." He grabs my wrist, hauling me off the dance floor in an instant.

"Rhodes!" I admonish. "What are you doing?"

"Kidnapping you."

"Taking me to your big, dark castle."

"Later. But for now…" He wrenches a door open, peering inside. "This will have to do."

"I am *not* going into a storage closet with you."

"You are too."

"Am not."

He takes a threatening step toward me, and I have to tip my head back to meet his heated stare. "Has anyone ever told you that you argue too much, Ryan? Someone really ought to spank you for it."

His words from our night in Vegas send a spark through me, and I arch a challenging brow. "Are you offering?"

"Yes." He takes another step, his lips ghosting along my ear. "Now, get in the closet…*wife*."

He doesn't have to say it again.

THE END

OTHER TITLES BY TEAGAN HUNTER

CAROLINA COMETS SERIES

Puck Shy

Blind Pass

One-Timer (Coming March 2022)

ROOMMATE ROMPS SERIES

Loathe Thy Neighbor

Love Thy Neighbor

Crave Thy Neighbor

Tempt Thy Neighbor

SLICE SERIES

A Pizza My Heart

I Knead You Tonight

Doughn't Let Me Go

A Slice of Love

Cheesy on the Eyes

TEXTING SERIES

Let's Get Textual

I Wanna Text You Up

Can't Text This

Text Me Baby One More Time

INTERCONNECTED STANDALONES

We Are the Stars

If You Say So

HERE'S TO SERIES

Here's to Tomorrow

Here's to Yesterday

Here's to Forever: A Novella

Here's to Now

Want to be part of a fun reader group, gain access to exclusive content and giveaways, and get to know me more?

Join Teagan's Tidbits on Facebook

Stay on top of my new releases!

Sign up for my newsletter

ACKNOWLEDGMENTS

The Marine. You're it for me and I can't imagine a life without you in it. Thank you for being the one constant in my life I can always count on.

Laurie. There is no doubt in my mind that I wouldn't be where I am today without you. Thanks for always kicking my ass when I need it.

My mom and sisters. I love you.

My editing team. Thank you for always squeezing me in and giving me a manuscript I can be proud of.

#soulmate. JUST BREATH. (iykyk)

The St. Louis Blues. Thank you for hours of entertainment. Sometimes you make me scream at my TV and sometimes you make me smile so damn big. Thanks for the rollercoaster ride. Now let's get another Cup, huh?

The Bloggers and Bookstagrammers and BookTok. You make this job a better one. Thank you for continued support. I appreciate you so much more than I could ever express properly.

My Tidbits. Thanks for giving me a safe space and always having my back. I owe you so much.

Reader. I was terrified to release a hockey romance because it was so out of my norm, but you showed up for the Carolina Comets and Blind Pass wouldn't be what it is without you. Thanks for going on this new adventure with me.

With love and unwavering gratitude,
Teagan

TEAGAN HUNTER is a Missouri-raised gal, but currently lives in South Carolina with her Marine veteran husband, where she spends her days begging him for a cat. She survives off of coffee, pizza, and sarcasm. When not writing, you can find her binge-watching *Supernatural* or *One Tree Hill.* She enjoys cold weather, buys more paperbacks than she'll ever read, and never says no to brownies.

www.teaganhunterwrites.com

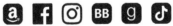

CPSIA information can be obtained
at www.ICGtesting.com
Printed in the USA
BVHW080257040123
655462BV00002B/387

9 781737 548171